ANCIENTS AND ANARCHY

BEAUTIFUL BEASTS ACADEMY

KIM FAULKS

MILA YOUNG

CONTENTS

Foreword   v
Ancients and Anarchy   vii

Chapter 1   1
Chapter 2   11
Chapter 3   20
Chapter 4   28
Chapter 5   39
Chapter 6   50
Chapter 7   61
Chapter 8   69
Chapter 9   80
Chapter 10   88
Chapter 11   97
Chapter 12   105
Chapter 13   113
Chapter 14   119
Chapter 15   126
Chapter 16   133
Chapter 17   140

Epilogue - Chapter One   147
Epilogue - Chapter Two   155
Epilogue - Chapter three   163
Finale... but not the end!   171
Halloween Special   173
BRAND NEW!   175

FOREWORD

Well...here it is. The last book in an epic series. We just wanted to steal your attention for just a second. We wanted to say we love you. We know that most of you came to this series with different expectations, some wanted the romance. That's what some readers wanted more of and we hope we gave that to you.

But see, the romance was secondary. Sure we love hunky wolves with kissable lips and abs that ripple for days. But for us that was always secondary to the real theme, and that was women, standing with women.

That was sisters uplifting sisters. That was knowing that you may not always agree, Hell, you may not always like each other. But who else knows what it's like under your skin? Who else knows what it's like to be a woman right here, and right now.

Who else knows how much love and hope you have inside you?

We do.

Us.

Me.

Your sister.
Your friend.
Mor and Ava.
And Nesrin with her catty snarl.
Crimsyn too, Salome, and Huntleigh.
They're waiting for you.
Let's fight this last battle together.
You with us?

Love
Mila and Kim, a.k.a Kila Foung

ANCIENTS AND ANARCHY

One man stands between the barbaric rule of Supernatural Council and the weakening line of the Ancients—my father, Dante Livingstone.

The time for peace is over. Swords have been drawn, and we stand at the edge of war.
I've fought Demons. I've battled lies. I survived with those I love standing beside me. But this time it's not enough. This time I'm up against a force not even Hekate can help me win.
I'm falling on my knees, desperate to find a way out of the dark. I don't want to believe it's over...I can't...not until the very end.

Read the gripping conclusion of the Beautiful Beasts Series today!

CHAPTER ONE

CHAOS REIGNS

STEEL GLINTED IN THE DARK AS THE BLADE SLIPPED ITS sheath. I was caught by the grinding sound, trapped by the shine of the weapon, unable to move.

"Are you aware of the consequences of these actions?" The voice boomed high above me.

I flinched with the sound as Dad took a step closer.

And in this moment, I couldn't breathe. Trapped with terror…

"Yes," Dad answered and lifted his gaze. "I'm aware of the actions."

"Dante," the Ancient, Vlad Vasile murmured beside him. "I'm begging you. This is madness, this is suicide. You're all that stands in their way. You give in and we all perish."

"Quiet!" That voice roared high above.

My knees trembled, fingers icy cold as they curled into fists. Still I forced my gaze to rise, forced myself to see the Council for what it truly was.

It *was* madness.

It was cruelty.

It *was* hate, hiding behind a mask. "No," I answered. "This is not happening." I took a step forward, breaking the suffocating grip of fear. "I won't allow this to happen."

More steel surrounded me. Blades and guns and shining silver eyes. There was a snarl from a Wolf I didn't know, and a whimper from my own father.

I'd end this right here, finish this once and for all. I turned my head, finding Thorin and Brylee, knowing that this has been the destination all along. The killing and the pain...especially to those I loved. This was what the Council wanted, this was how they used and manipulated.

"I want to make a deal," I answered.

"Morwenna, *do not say one more word*." There was fear in Dad's voice, real crippling fear.

I turned my head toward him. His eyes were wide, a sheen of sweat against a perfect brow.

"You don't understand what's happening," he whispered and cast a panicked gaze toward the Vampire sitting high above us.

"Enough!" The leader of the Council roared.

I flinched and jerked my gaze to where he stood. He was young, younger than I'd imagined, barely two hundred years old, and he sat in more power than I could ever hope to.

"Morwenna Livingstone, you are stripped of your title of Understudy." He glanced at Dad. "And are hereby..."

A savage whimper slipped from Dad's lips. "*No....*"

A roar followed, bellowing and brutal. Steps thundered from my right as Chuck lifted his hand. Steel glinted. The gun was all I saw as he lifted the muzzle to the young Judge sitting high above us.

I jerked my gaze to Dad, waiting for him to roar a

command to *stop!* But he didn't. He didn't say anything at all. Just watched as Chuck squeezed the trigger.

Boom! The sound shattered the eerie silence.

The bitter scent of gunpowder filled the air. Movement dragged my gaze to the Ancient as he lifted his hand and gave the command, and in a war-cry that filled the massive room, the Ancient's warriors were a tsunami as they charged forward. The thunder of their boots filled the room.

Chuck squeezed off three more shots as Dad gripped my arm. "Move, Morwenna...*now.*"

I stumbled forward unable to tear my gaze from the avalanche of Council's warriors charging toward us...with the Vampire, Slayer, in front.

Slayer threw his sword like an axe, the tip turning end over end until it found its mark. Chuck cried out, stumbled and then went down.

"No!" I screamed and lunged forward.

But the room was chaos. Screams and slaughter mingled with the *crack* of gunshots. I turned, grasping Dad's hand, dragging him with me. "Dad, come on!"

But one look into his eyes and I saw the truth. He'd known what he was walking into. He knew this would happen. He knew it all. Dark eyes glinted, his focus slipping past me. I followed his gaze as Slayer roared forward, and behind a wall of Vampires, Chuck rose.

Blood soaked his white shirt. He lifted his hand, grip steady and squeezed the trigger...*boom...boom...boom!* The gun never kicked in his grip, only glinted as he charged.

"Take Morwenna!" Dad roared. "Keep her safe."

Chuck swung his gaze to me, and then glanced to Dad. But my father was already turning, already shoving me between the surge of Vampires as the head of the Supernatural Council rose to his feet and screamed above us. "Get them! *Get them now!*"

Strong hands grabbed me, pulling me away as Dad reached inside his jacket and dragged free a shining silver Ruger, took aim and then fired.

"Dad!" I screamed and lunged.

But Chuck's grip was a vise, holding me in place as Dad swung the muzzle of the weapon to the head of the Supernatural Council and fired once more.

"We have to go!" Chuck roared in my ears.

But I couldn't...I couldn't leave him... *not like this.* I swung my gaze to my bodyguard. *"You have to save him! You have to save my dad!"*

I'd never seen Chuck scared before, never seen him so much as rattled. But his dark Vampire eyes widened, the tiny shake of his head was more for him than it was for me.

I yanked on his hold as the savage clash of guns and blades rang out. The Ancient stood in the middle, watching as his men fought the Council.

And one by one they fell, blood spurted into the air from a neck wound, another grabbed his chest and toppled at Vlad's feet as the *boom* from a shotgun rang out.

"Morwenna...*we have to go.*" Chuck yanked my arm, lifting me from my feet.

I'd fought in battle.

I'd succumbed to war.

But this was no fight...*this was a massacre.*

Death was everywhere...in their eyes and their screams. "Dad come on!" I yelled, searching for pale skin and midnight eyes.

But he was gone, lost to the sea of darkness, and across the clash of steel Slayer rose to his feet, his face splattered with another's blood. He lifted his hand, the muzzle of the gun pointed at me.

But it wasn't me, not really, and those feral eyes weren't locked on mine...they were gripped by Chuck's.

"You can't escape your past forever, Hunter," Slayer barked. "Everyone you love will finally see you for the monster you really are."

Chuck gave a snarl and swung the muzzle of his gun high before he squeezed the trigger.

Slayer jerked with the impact, blood spreading across his shoulder as the Ancient stumbled forward, his dark eyes seized mine as he screamed, *"Go now!"*

I was dragged backwards, slipping through the massacre around me, until the rush of the dying and the dead stole everything away.

"We have to go back!" I yanked on Chuck's hold. "Chuck! *Chuck! We have to go back!"*

But he was a locomotive, shooting a Council Vampire as he rushed toward us. "We get out of here, Mor. Any way we damn well can."

Not without Dad.

Tears blurred. This was all my fault. If I hadn't gone to that damn school. If I hadn't touched those goddamn diamonds.

Screams filled my ears and raked claws along my soul. I plunged into the darkness inside my chest, to that faint flicker of power that lingered inside me. *Please, Hekate. Hear me, please hear me. I need you...*

Chuck grabbed me around the waist and lifted my feet from the floor, swinging me to protect me with his body as a Vampire charged. The deafening sound of gunshots and screams were all I heard until the sickening *crunch* of the impact.

I swayed in Chuck's arms as he stumbled. Momentum took us, carrying us away from the eye of this terrifying storm and away from my father.

"Dad!" I screamed. *"DAD!"*

But he was gone, and then so were we, sinking into the darkness of the Council's chambers. Chuck stumbled, his knee gave way, sending me sprawling. I hit the ground hard, pain lashed my knee until I shoved upwards, grasping Chuck under the arms. "I've got you," I roared.

And then I saw it, the blade lodged hilt deep into his chest.

"Go." He shoved me. "Run, Morwenna."

Agony sparkled in his eyes, and the sight of that was my own blade. My heart gave a tremor, squeezing and clenching, driving the poison of pain through my veins. "No." I shook my head. "Not without you."

I tore my gaze from the blade in his chest and grasped him around the waist. My legs shuddered, nerves were frayed. I prayed to anyone who'd hear me, anyone who'd help me.

"You!"

I glanced to my right as Brylee stepped from the darkness. She was covered in blood...someone else's blood. The splattering covered her face, blending in with her freckles. She lifted her hand, fingers now turned into claws.

Chuck groaned, the sound was raw and painful as he lifted his hand. The muzzle of the gun danced in the air, moving from the center of her chest, to the chaos behind.

She took a step closer, her eyes not on the weapon, but on me. "You know how long I've waited for this moment?"

My grasp slipped around his waist as Brylee stepped closer. Heavy breaths made her chest swell. I glanced around us, to the dark, stony walls...and the closed door that seemed too far away.

I gripped my bodyguard against me and turned. It was my turn to protect him now. My turn to put my body on the line.

"No little friends to protect you now," she murmured. Amber eyes sparkled with malice.

Chuck gave a whimper as his hand shook violently and then dropped to his side, taking the protection of the gun with it.

There was nothing I could do now, no prayers to be whispered, no loyal friends to stand with me. I'd tried. Tried as hard as I could—*and I'd failed*. I glanced to the bloodshed and mayhem, and then back to Brylee.

She smiled a sickening smile.

I have something for you, Chuck's voice filled my mind as Brylee took a step closer.

She raised her hand, claws still dripping with blood. One swipe and I lunged backwards, shoving Chuck behind me.

"Can't duck and weave forever," she murmured. "I've dreamt of this moment, wondering what it'd feel like to take down Morwenna Livingstone."

She circled, her eyes fixed on me as I swapped one arm around Chucks waist for the other.

"Go." He pushed me away. "I'll hold her off. You need to run."

But there was no running, not anymore. I'd left one Father behind. I glanced to the wave of Vampires as they cleaved and fought each other.

But the past wasn't done, Chuck's words slipping from the past into the present once more. *The tip is tainted with something deadly should you need it.*

And as Brylee lifted her hand into the air, I reached for my hair. Her battle cry was savage and fierce, amber eyes burning orange as she lunged, clawing the air inches from my face.

I grasped the silver pin from my hair and swung. Chuck gave a grunt and yanked me backwards, narrowly missing the swipe of her claws. Air buffeted my face, casting the strands of my hair aside as they tumbled around my face.

"Fucking *bitch!*" Brylee screamed and corrected her balance.

She'd missed.

But I didn't.

The tiny scratch on her arm welled with a single drop of blood. She sucked in a hard breath and then glanced to the dagger shaped pin in my hand, and then slowly glanced to the scratch on her arm. "You honestly thought that was going to save you?" She lifted her head. "You truly are p-pathetic-c."

But the last word slurred.

She swayed on her feet, brows furrowed with a look of confusion. "What?" She tried to form a sentence. "What did you do to me?"

I reached up with one hand, and gently slid the pin into my hair once more, careful not to gouge my scalp. "I fought you," I answered turning away from her. "With the love of my friends once more."

I grasped Chuck as he shook and shuddered. Sweat slipped into his eyes as his gaze met mine and lifted his arm.

"And this time I won," I murmured without taking my gaze off him.

I reached my hand around, gripping under his arms as the heavy *thud* came from behind me. I shuffled forward, slowing as one of the Ancient's Vampires lunged in front of us, taking down one of the Council's blood drenched men.

We stumbled and swayed, keeping to the shadows and inched toward the door. Bodies were piled in the middle. I caught a glimpse of the Ancient as the Council's men shackled him and shoved him forward.

"They won't kill him," Chuck whispered.

I heaved one more step closer to the door and met his gaze. "Are you willing to bet his life on that?"

"We were..." he answered.

I knew then, knew as I shifted my grip and reached for the door. They knew this would happen...they knew it all. The poisoned dagger hair pin. The quiet control, stopping me as I spoke my mind.

"You need to leave this place," a snarl came from in front of us.

One of the Ancient's men guarded the door. His clothes were blood-soaked, the blade in his hand still dripped red. He took a step closer, glancing from me to Chuck. "You get her out, warrior. That was the deal."

One nod from Chuck was all I needed. Tears sprang to my eyes as I stumbled forward. The Ancient's Vampire reached for the lock of the door. No one was allowed to leave, not unless the Ancient wanted them too.

And it looked like he wanted us too. The *snap* of the bolts filled my ears as I walked Chuck closer. The door opened wide. I looked over my shoulder one last time, seeing them lead the chained Ancient through a doorway on the other side of the room.

Slayer reached out and shoved Vlad forward, and then followed.

"We have to go," Chuck growled. "But we'll be back...*soon.*"

We stepped through the doorway, listening to the grind of the hinges before it closed with a *bang* behind us.

It felt like a year since I'd stepped through that doorway and faced the Supernatural Council.

It felt like a year of fighting.

A year of terror, and as I gripped Chuck and we stumbled along the hallway to the world outside, I knew I'd never forget what happened here, not as long as I lived.

Tears slipped down my cheeks as we hurried.

I was coming back.

I'd find my dad...

And then I'd find the one they called the Judge.

And I'd tear him apart.

Rage filled me, plunging me into the icy depths of my power. I gripped Chuck, and focused on that doorway, and then outside to the car. Judas and Ava filled my mind.

Find them, the urgency whispered.

And I would...even if I had to drive all night.

CHAPTER TWO

IN CASE OF EMERGENCY

THE CITY LIGHTS GLINTED IN THE DARKNESS. CHUCK had been silent for most of the ride, slumped sideways on the back seat where he fell.

"Hold on Chuck, *hold on.*"

Silence answered, but inside my head all I heard were screams. The night had never felt so hostile to me before, never so...*lonely*. I sucked in a hard breath as tears slipped down my cheeks. I could do this. I could do this.

I could....

A tortured sound slipped from my lips, like an animal in pain. Only I was that animal. I felt lost, abandoned. I felt like I stood on the other side of a gaping divide. I didn't know how to find my way back to where the others waited. I turned my head and glanced at Chuck slumped on the back seat and my hands trembled on the wheel.

Come on Mor, just make it. I focused on the road and the trees, I tried to remember the direction we'd driven. But it was hard when you sat in the backseat, glancing at the blur of trees through a darkened window.

You can do this, Judas' voice filled my head.

We're right with you, Ava followed.

I could feel them, and it was that feeling I held onto. It was that feeling I fought for. I stared at the road and then fumbled for my phone.

My phone...what if they were tracking me?

My breath caught. I jerked my gaze to Chuck, soundless in the back seat. *What if they were tracking the both of us?* I gripped the wheel, leaned forward and scanned the night sky.

They could be out there. They could be hunting us now. I jerked the wheel and pumped the brakes, swinging the limousine to the shoulder of the road.

My heart gave a shudder as I shoved open the driver's door and reached for my cell phone. Fingers trembled as I shoved the back of the case open and pulled the phone apart, searching for the sim card. One snap and it was broken. I dropped the pieces to the ground and crushed them under my heel before I lunged for the back of the car.

"Chuck," I called his name as I yanked the handle. "If you can hear me, a little help would be perfect right about now."

I leaned closer, searching the outside of his jacket and then the inside. His eyes fluttered open for a second.

"Good, you're not dead," I muttered, adding a touch of sarcasm.

It was all I had to hold onto, all I had to keep me from crumbling apart. My hands skimmed something hard. I delved inside and yanked his phone free.

He gave a mumble, and then a slow hiss of a breath. His eyes fluttered open once more, but there was panic inside them...and fear.

"Hideeee."

The word was a slow hiss, making me still. I swallowed, met his gaze. "Where? Where do I hide?"

His eyes closed, chest sank with the exhale. I dragged the phone free and then stared at him. *Hide?* I straightened with his phone in my hand. The word resounded, and panic swiftly followed filling me until it was all I could think about, all I could feel...I stumbled backwards and fumbled with his phone, opening the case to see the screen.

A tiny piece of paper floated from a pocket on the side of his case. I caught the flutter, snatching it before it hit the ground.

Mor.
In case of Emergency.

I sucked in a breath and opened the paper. There were numbers...a whole row of numbers. Tears blurred the sight. I swiped the trickle as they fell, the paper falling onto the seat. Headlights splashed the asphalt behind us. I sucked in a hard breath and stumbled away from the open doorway, terror inching its way to the surface of my mind.

I glanced to Chuck laying helpless in the back of the car as the headlight grew brighter. The car was slowing as it crested the rise behind us. I lunged for the backseat and searched for a weapon.

If the Council found us then they wouldn't send just one warrior...

They'd send them all...

I skimmed my fingers under the backseat and then along the side of the limousine. Crystal glass clinked as I glanced through the back window to the headlights outside.

The car slowed, tires crunched. All I could hear was

that sound and Chuck's desperate plea ringing in my head...*hideee*.

My fingers skimmed cold steel. I jerked my gaze to the glasses and felt underneath. It was a shotgun, sawn-off at the handle. I gripped what was left of the stock and tore it free as the car slowed right behind us. Steel smacked my thigh as I straightened.

The whir of a window made my stomach clench.

"Honey, you okay out here?" a man called out.

I stared into the car to the faint spill of dashboard lights. He was older, white hair and kind eyes...traveling with his wife. I lowered my hand, dropping the shotgun to the floor of the car. "Yes, Sir. Thank you. Just needed a breather, wake myself up a little."

"You be careful along these roads." His wife leaned over to call through the window. "But if you need a pick me up, Hannie's Diner is about five minutes' drive thatta way. Careful now, Hunters Call is a dangerous town after dark."

Hideee...the word resounded as I followed her finger to the faint sparkle of lights in the distance. I was so consumed with finding my way back to the city I never thought about anywhere else.

"How far is Tricks City from here?" I glanced their way.

"About thirty minutes," the old man answered. "Hunters is the last stop between here and there. You be careful going into the city. It's all over the news tonight."

I flinched as a chill raced along my spine as I murmured. "What's all over the news?"

"The riots honey," the old woman answered. "The city is burning."

I glanced to the darkness as that feeling of terror grew inside me. The city was burning...*my city*.

Hide, Chuck's warning gripped me. I stepped backwards and closed the door. "Thank you. I think I'll head to that diner after all."

The old man gave a nod and then a small smile. "Well okay, if you're sure you're okay we'll head on home."

"Thank you," I murmured and stumbled toward the open driver's door. "Thank you so much."

The words slipped from my lips. But I was already racing toward that town inside my head, already searching for somewhere to hide—just long enough to call those I loved.

I slipped behind the wheel as the old couple drove on by, leaving the limousine bathed in the red glow of their tail lights. I shoved the limousine into gear and pulled out, following them until I caught the sign for Hunters Call.

Desperation urged me faster. I shoved my foot against the accelerator and sped toward the town. Faint lights sparkled as the trees gave way to wide roads and darkened shops along the main street. True to their word a diner was alight further toward the heart of the town.

The sleek black limousine stuck out amongst rusted pick-up trucks and ancient four wheel drives. I needed to hide, and sitting outside a brightly lit diner in this thing wasn't the answer.

I eased off the accelerator and cruised through the green street light. The diner was busy, families sat in booths, men and women sat on stools at the counter. I stared until the place slipped by. I need somewhere darker, somewhere busy with lots of people...somewhere I could blend in.

Red and purple lights caught my focus down the darkened side street. I tapped on the brake, slowing the car, and then hit the turn signal as I jerked the wheel. "Please be okay...please be okay..." The place looked dark and seedy.

Live Girls, flashed neon red. "Okay, not the most respectable place I could find."

The darkened alley next to the seedy motel was wide enough for me to nose the limo inside. Women were dressed in knee-high pleather boots wearing nothing more than a scrap of cloth to cover their breasts and hug their hips. One of them lifted her head as I nosed the limo into the alley and then started to stride toward us, leaving the others behind.

I pulled in far enough to hide the rear of the car from the street and then killed the engine. A gasping, wheezing sound came from Chuck. I winced at the sound, and then shoved from the driver's seat as the woman stepped into the alley. "Hey Princess, you heading to a party?"

"No," I answered and then reached into my pocket. "But I'll give you twenty for watching out for anyone suspicious." I peeled off a note from the small wad and shoved the rest into my pocket.

She eyed me up and down, stilling at my chest. "You in some kind of trouble, honey?"

I swallowed hard and then looked down. Blood splatter marred my shirt, spreading across my chest. The more I looked the more I saw. I swiped the back of my hand against the seat of my pants, still it was everywhere...

Screams filled my head, and the bitter foul scent of blood followed, in an instant I was back in that room, fighting for my life as the Supernatural Council waged war. "Yeah," I answered without thinking. "I guess you could say I am."

She glanced at the limo. "What do you need?"

I flinched, bringing myself into the present once more. "I need to hide, just for a little while, and some place I can call my friends. They'll come for me, they'll help."

One nod of her head was all that was needed. She

turned her head, lifted her hand, placing two fingers in her mouth and whistled. The sharp call echoed through the alley.

"Georgette, we need a little help here," she called.

Barely a breath later there were more. Their heels clattering as they stepped from the pavement into the alley.

"Our girlfriend here needs a shirt, something less...*bloody.*" My guardian angel turned to me and smiled. "Honey, you escort her into Raider's, she needs to use the phone to call her friends."

My throat tightened. I couldn't speak. I swallowed the lump in the back of my throat as one of the women dropped her hand to her shirt and started to work the buttons.

Tears filled my eyes. I blinked and looked away.

"Aww precious, don't cry."

I shook my head and then turned to her once more. "I don't even know your name."

"They call me Hart," my rescuer answered as Georgette slipped off her long sleeved black shirt and handed it over.

"Thank you," I murmured and took the shirt.

"You go, sweetheart." Hart motioned with her head toward the bright flashing lights. "Me and the girls will keep an eye on whoever you have in that car."

In a terrifying vision I saw Chuck coming to with mortal women around him. Would he lash out? Would he think he was in danger? "Whatever you do, don't open the door. We're not...we're not safe."

Hart took a step and leaned closer. "Who the Hell is this day and age? Hurry now. Don't you worry about your friend. They'll be fine."

I hurried, yanking on the shirt over my blood splattered top and took a step toward the friend she called Honey. She turned, stepped up onto the pavement, and led me toward the flashing sign of the Motel.

The reception was alight, and big, leading to the long row of rooms that stretched as far as they alley we left behind.

"This way, babe." Honey motioned me forward and made for the bright glaring lights. Cars drove in behind us. Headlights splashed against my back. I counted three before I turned my focus on the reception.

The bell above the doorway gave a *ding* as I stepped inside. A fat, balding man rose up from a chair behind the counter as the drone of a TV filled the room.

"Gary, we need to use the phone," Honey muttered and then leaned over the counter to reach for the handset. "You don't mind, do you precious?"

The guy shook his head, he was too busy staring at her breasts as they bulged out of her top. She smiled and gave him a wink, reaching around to hand me the phone. "That's what I figured sugar. Say, have you lost weight?"

The diversion was all for me. I grasped the phone and quickly punched in the number and waited. The call buzzed...ringing...ringing...ringing. "Please pick up...it's me...*it's me.*"

"Yeah?" The deep growl cut through the line.

"Oh thank God," I whispered and gripped the handset.

"Mor, is that you?" Judas answered.

Relief swept through me as the fragile words slipped from my lips. "Judas, I'm in trouble."

Savage snarls echoed in the background. Nero and Bond, I knew. "Baby, tell me where you are."

I closed my eyes as the words spilled free. "There was no hearing, Judas. They didn't want to hear from us at all. It was an ambush...it was all an ambush."

A tortured moan cut through the ear piece. "Tell me where you are, Morwenna. I'm coming to get you."

"There's a motel in Hunters Call about thirty minutes west of the city."

The frantic thud of steps echoed through the speaker. Judas wasn't just coming for me...*he was running*.

"Stay right there, you hear me? Stay right there. *I'm on my way.*"

Silence carried down the line. I pulled the phone away from my ear and stared at the *end call*...flashing on the tiny screen. Honey turned toward me, glanced at the phone and then gently took it from my hands. "Gary, you, kind Sir, are a gentleman."

She fussed and flirted, but inside I was already out in that dark alley...already waiting for my Wolves to come.

And they were coming.

They were coming for me

Nothing would stop them now.

CHAPTER THREE

DESPERATE TIMES

THE WORLD SEEMED TO BE SLOWLY DISAPPEARING around me. I'd always thought I had life under control, that things would work out... but it was all an illusion... a load of shit. Everything I'd ever known had been ripped out from under me and for the life of me I couldn't see a way to crawl out of this mess.

I paced across the mouth of a dark alleyway, my footfalls hitting asphalt, the sound masked by police sirens in the distance and the rowdy cheers from a nearby bar. The angels who'd helped me earlier left me alone to wait for my Wolves. That was the only thing keeping me glued in one piece... knowing they were coming.

I'd made the mistake of thinking I could do it on my own... not again... *never again.*

The smell of take-out pizza from nearby shops made my stomach roll.

I kicked a trash can in my stride until movement caught my attention from the parking lot. The lamppost tossed shadows over the half empty spaces, white reversing lights glowed in the night, and I released the breath trapped in my chest.

Back and forth, back and forth. I let momentum take me, just for a moment, my arms wrapped around my middle. But with the movement came the memories, and the screams.

The sounds would haunt me for the rest of my immortal life.

We'd been betrayed.

I tried not to think of Dad, tried not to think of the Ancient. They wouldn't hurt them...wouldn't do anything to incite a war. The thought was the only thing keeping me together. I turned from the moss covered brick wall of the alley and paced alongside the limo once more.

The growl of an engine erupted, and I spun around. A sports car pulled into the parking space with speed, hugging the corner tight. Dark tinted windows concealed the driver, but I knew all three of them were inside. I knew it, and my heart galloped. I was racing toward them and reached the driver's door before the car's engine cut. Every nerve in my body buzzed with the anticipation of being with them in a way that was more than tangible.

The door swung open and Judas climbed from the shadows, stealing my breath and igniting the fire in my heart.

I jumped into his arms, burying my face into the warmth of his neck. Emotions rolled through me, they throttled me, and the tears fell. It felt like I'd carried the world on my shoulders for so long, and I was tired of trying to be strong alone... it was my fault I know that for pushing others away.

Judas looped me into his embrace, his breath in my ears. "We're here now." He lifted me off my feet and walked us to the sidewalk before he set me down. Nero and Bond were at my side, all three encasing me, protecting me.

"Mor," Ava called out, and I broke free from Judas to find her running from the sports car.

My heart leapt at seeing her, and she rushed toward me, until we clashed in a tangle of arms and hugs. "I've been so fucking scared for you," she mumbled.

I turned to find all four of them surrounding me, and excitement radiated through me... it was pure adrenaline and energy.

Ava's arms were animated as she spoke. "I've been pacing a hole in my room with worry."

Judas' hands cupped my face and he made me look up at him, while his thumbs wiped away the tears. "Are you hurt?"

I shook my head. "No, but Chuck...he's bad." I pointed to the limousine.

Ava gasped and darted into the limo's back door.

Judas studied me. Fury burned behind his gaze... Not at me, but the fucked up situation.

"What's our plan?" Bond asked, his hand on my mine, fingers intertwined, reminding me I was no longer alone in this tangled mess.

"*Oh my God!* There's so much blood." Ava's voice tightened as she climbed out of the limo and stared back inside at Chuck. When she glanced my way, dread crossed her gaze.

"I can fix this. I can heal him," I explained. "But we gotta get out of here. It's not safe. It's not...*safe.*"

Her eyes grew watery. She swallowed, and then swallowed again, turning to look at the limousine once more.

I reached for her, grabbing her hand as it fluttered to her mouth. I needed this, just as much as she did. My arms went around her. I dragged her against my chest. Just a second. Just to stop from falling apart. We held each other, until my Wolves joined in.

It was us against the world.

Hate rolled through me like a tempest storm.

"What are we meant to do now?" Ava asked, pulling away from our embrace. "Track down your dad, break him out?"

"I don't know. But it's not that easy. Whatever is happening is so much bigger than I first thought. The Ancient is caught up in it, the human council, the supernaturals. And they'll be coming after me."

"They can try." Judas brown eyes sparked with danger.

"So, we need a place to lay low," Bond muttered. "Somewhere to think things through."

"They'll search everywhere and everyone." I held his gaze. "No one is safe. Not anymore."

"Has to be somewhere they can't reach." Judas growled and turned away.

And just as the last words fell from his lips, I remembered Chuck's note that fell out of my phone in the limo.

Mor.
In case of Emergency.

I stepped from the tangle of arms, and hurried toward the midnight car once more. Chuck's note filled my mind. I yanked the door handle and lunged inside, searching the passenger's seat.

"What are you looking for?" Ava asked from behind me.

"It's gotta be here. I just know it is." I kneeled down and pressed my hand in between the seat and middle console, when my fingers touched the thin slice of paper. "Yes, I got you." I dug deeper and with two fingers and pulled the sucker free.

Climbing out of the car, I stared at the handwritten numbers running across the top.

"What is it? A phone number?" Ava asked, and the Wolves closed in, staring down at the note in my hand.

I shook my head. "Too many numbers. Chuck placed this note in my phone case for emergencies. It has to mean something."

"Let me look at that." Bond reached over and took the paper from my hand. He pulled out his phone and was tapping away, while Ava shrugged toward me.

"If anyone can work it out, it's Bond," Nero muttered. "The guy's some kind of puzzle guru."

I hoped he worked it out. Judas nodded, reaffirming Nero's confidence.

"Coordinates," Bond blurted out and looked up. "These are GPS directions to a location, and I know exactly where it is." He lifted his phone, showing us a map and the red dot pointed to a spot right in the middle of Tricks city.

"What's the location?" Ava took his phone and studied the map.

"Somewhere Chuck though I'd be safe when I faced an emergency," I murmured.

"Then we go there," Judas added.

"We go there now," I reiterated.

Without any words, Bond got into the driver's seat and me in the passenger's, while Judas and Nero rushed back to the sports car. I glanced into the back seat of the limo to where Ava lifted Chuck's head and cradled it in her lap. She pushed strands of hair off his face. She adored him so much.

"I hope you're right," Ava said, doubt threading her

words, but I felt the same. So much had gone wrong recently, and I had to believe Chuck's note would help.

"Me too." I pulled the belt across my body and buckled in while Bond started the engine with the keys I'd left in the ignition.

He pulled away from the curb near the dark alley, and before long we merged onto the main road. Through the side mirror, Judas' sports car stayed close behind us. I sat back, pressed into the seat, my shaky hands tucked under my thighs. Outside, night claimed everything, and only the occasional streetlight illuminated the shop fronts we passed. Soon, we left the town behind and open fields flanked our passage, swallowed by darkness.

Bond's hand found my thigh, his touch scorching, and he looked over, shadows crowded under his eyes. But his smile softened his features. "We'll get through this."

"Hell, yeah," Ava butted in from the back. "After all the shit we've already been through, I'm gonna go Kraken on anyone's ass who stands in our way."

I burst out laughing, picturing her tentacles slapping and whacking the Council. If only it was that easy to fix the problems. We kept driving for the next hour, a false sense of calm joining us, until the city lights rose from the horizon up ahead.

Stiffening in my seat, I stared out at Tricks, at the gray smoke curling upward from golden flames somewhere deep in the city. "What's burning?" As the words left my mouth, I recalled what those two old people who helped me had said. The city was on fire. This must be what they were talking about.

Bond hit the radio button. A rock band played. He kept changing the stations but no one was talking about the flames. Once we reached the city, cars and people were everywhere, and the stench of burning wood clogged the air. Bond flipped on the air conditioner, and we crept deeper into the city, following Chuck's coordinates.

The closer we got, the more smoke curled around the buildings. Sirens filled the night, and behind us, flashing blue and red lights pulsed through the smoke. The acrid stench slithered into the car, stinging my eyes until they teared up.

Around the next corner, the cars were at a snail's pace, and I peered down a long street. At the very end, a loft building burned, black smoke billowing out from the windows, the roof was half fall in, and orange flames, garish against the black building... Several men in bright red cloaks with pointed hoods were smashing part of the building, helping bring it down faster.

I choked on the smell, and the shock rattled through me.

"Aren't they wearing the hood of the Supernatural Council?" Ava murmured.

My head whirred, but I looked around us to work out where we were in the city. The deli at the corner, the bank across the road, and small park to our left. And I knew this place... My stomach dropped down to my feet.

"Fuck! They're burning down the Ancient's temple," I blurted and learned closer to the door, my palm splayed against the glass. "The supernatural council are tearing it down."

I wanted to throw up.

Long flames licked the air, consuming the tower I'd visited with Dad when I was younger.

The pulsing police lights drew close behind us, and Bond veered out of the way for them to pass. The moment they curved onto the road, the culprits ran into the shadows leaving behind the inferno. Their threat clear.

This wasn't the only temple they'd burned down... I knew it... knew that the others across the city had been targeted as well.

My mind filled with images from the hearing, the battle that was about so much more than me. This had everything to do with a struggle between the Supernatural Council and Vampires, and I'd just ended up caught in the middle of the battle and delivered my dad and Vlad right into their hands. My fingers curled into fists, my nails digging into flesh. Dread churned in my stomach.

"We need to get out of here fast," Ava called from the back seat.

Bond swung the steering wheel and rushed us down a side road, away from the fire. We took so many turns, I lost track of where we were, but when we finally came to a stop, I lifted my head. We were parked in a back alley behind the rear of buildings with a lofty metal fence on the other side. I peered out to see a small house cloaked in darkness, windows barred with wooden planks, the place derelict and rundown.

"You sure this is the place from Chuck's coordinates?" I asked and glanced back to see the sports car pull up behind us before Judas killed the lights.

"Stay here and I'll check it out." Bond climbed out of the car, Judas and Nero doing the same behind us, the thump of their doors echoing around us.

"Do you think we'll be safe here?" Ava's voice trembled.

"I hope so." My muscles twitched with an impulse to run back to the temple and track down those responsible, make them pay for their crimes, make them give me my Dad back. But that wouldn't help anyone. Nowhere was safe... not now. Maybe not ever.

CHAPTER FOUR

BLEED ME DRY

Judas stepped out from the rear door of the boarded up house, the wind buffeting against him, tugging on his shirt. I climbed out of the limo and into the night, a bitter wind curling around my hair.

"It's all clear," he called.

Nero propped open the door wider to the house, waving me in. "Inside. We'll get Chuck."

Ava shook her head. "Not me. I want to help."

"You can help, as soon as we carry the big lug in here," he said softly. "We're going to take good care of him, Ava. Trust me."

Her eyes were wide with fear. I knew what tortured words filled her mind. This wasn't about me now, it was what she needed to do to stop from spiralling out of control.

I nodded. "We'll be waiting."

They left then. Judas giving me a quick glance, his eyes filled with fear.

Please be okay...please be okay...

Darkness enveloped us, along with a heavy stuffiness that clogged in my throat. At the end of the narrow corridor, a single flame flickered. A beacon calling to us, and we ran to it, emerging into a lounge room where a small TV with rabbit ears sat on a small wooden table. The fabric of the couch was of muted hues, and a table and four chairs that belonged to different sets filled the space beneath a window, while the carpet near the barren wall was lined with a folded bed sheet. Guns, knives, swords, rope, tape, and an array of other weapons lay in a perfect line. Including a pile of garbage bags.

"Whoa." Ava stepped closer and inspected them. "Do you think these are all Chuck's?"

"I'd say so."

She looked at me over her shoulder. "Who the Hell was he?"

"I have no idea," I murmured and stared at the weapons.

This wasn't the Chuck I knew. It was the house of a mercenary. A house of torture and death. A house of darkness. Anything could happen here. No one heard the screams. It offered Chuck sanctuary, and now it would offer us a location to lay low.

"I still love him," Ava murmured, staring at the weapons.

"He's still our Chuck." I answered, remembering the way he'd stepped into the line of fire to protect me during the hearing, how his body jarred from the blows. How he took the blade to the chest for me.

My throat thickened, hands trembled. "He'll always be our Chuck."

I needed to somehow push past the terror and the anguish, or it'd tear me apart.

But those images were locked tight like a fist inside me, and I felt like a hollow shell.

A loud gruff came from the hallway, and I turned to see Judas shuffling down the hall backward, holding onto Chuck's shoulders, while Bond carried his legs. Nero shut the door quickly behind them.

Ava and I stepped out of the way as they heaved him into the room and set him on the couch. He slumped on the brown cushions, his torn shirt gaping open, stained with blood.

"You need to heal him," Ava pleaded with me as she dropped to her knees near him, grasping his hand in hers.

I rolled up my sleeves and glanced at the wall of weapons before I crossed the room and picked up a hunter's blade. One side serrated, the other sharp.

"You sure about this?" Judas touched my arm.

"Please. *Mor*, hurry," Ava pleaded.

"It's the only way," I muttered and met Judas' gaze, shadows leaping across his face. "He needs fresh and powerful blood."

I pressed the blade against the line of my wrist, and then sliced deep. Pain lashed deep, nerves stinging in an instant.

Blood bubbled across the wound, running red over the meat of my palm and down my fingers. Judas took the knife as I fell to my knees.

His skin was so pale, lips nothing more than a slash on his face.

Ava moved to stand at the end of the couch at the top of his head and placed two hands on his face, tilting his head back. His jaw naturally opened a smidgen.

I placed my wrist over his mouth, and pressed the flesh hard against his teeth, willing every drop to find its way along his throat.

My blood was strong. But was it strong enough to heal someone like Chuck?

If it did, what would he feel? Would he sense that dark remnant of power inside my chest. Would he know my emotions, my fear...my desire?

I lifted my gaze to Judas as he watched me with panic. Blood dripped through ashen lips, like a stab wound in the snow. One drop crested the corner of his lips, and rolled across his cheek, leaving a crimson streak behind before it bled into the cushion beneath him.

I pressed my wrist harder against his mouth, willing the flow to hurry.

My Wolves stood around us, ready, and waiting for something to go wrong.

Please, come back, Chuck. Please.

The cut throbbed, stinging and pinching.

"How much longer?" Nero demanded.

"However long it takes," I murmured and pressed more blood into Chuck's mouth.

Ava patted down his hair, her eyes shut, her lips moving in silent prayer.

Shadows moved into the room, reaching for me before movement blurred at the end of my view.

"Mor! *Mor, that's enough.*" White fangs filled my view. Judas was so close, grasping my hand and wrenching it away.

Blood spilled down Chuck's chin.

Panic filled me, bleeding out of that darkness inside my mind. "No!" I lunged forward, the room so bright now. Sparks filled my view. Trails of blood over Chuck's lips was all I could see. "You wasted it..." I wrenched my gaze to Judas, lips curled as I roared. *"You wasted it!"*

"*Look at yourself!*" he roared. "Look at what you're doing. He's no good to us alive, if you're dead."

A moan tore through the room, low and guttural...

"Chuck?" Ava murmured. "*Chuck!*"

The room seemed to spin as I jerked my gaze to the Vampire who saved me.

His lids fluttered open, and then closed. A pinkened tongue skimmed darkening lips. "You guys always going to bitch and bicker?"

Hope fluttered in my chest, until pain tore across his face. His eyes snapped open, fangs pencil thin and needing. "More," he growled, wincing and moaning in pain. "I need more."

Strong hands gripped my wrist, jerking me forward as he bit.

Agony roared through my wrist. I tried to pull away. My free fist pummeled his face.

Still he held on, dark eyes glistening with need.

He wasn't the man I knew in this moment.

Not the Vampire.

Not the friend.

He was a beast, a monster desperate to survive.

"Stop!" Judas roared, one hand grasping my wrist while Bond and Nero grasped the Vampire.

"*Stop!*" Ava roared. "You try to tear him from her and he'll kill her. Can't you see? He's not Chuck. He's not the Vampire we know. He'll tear her apart to satiate his thirst."

She turned to him, lowering her voice. "Chuck...Chuck I know you can hear me."

A whimper slipped from my lips. My knees shuddered, locking in place. I turned to Judas, finding that glint of fear.

"Chuck, honey, it's Ava." Panic filled her words as she stole a glance my way and then moved closer to Chuck. "I know you can hear me and I need you listen to me right now. You need to let go, Chuck. It's Mor you're hurting. Do you hear me? *It's Mor.*"

Something flickered in his eyes. Recognition. Pain, and the glint of the beast slipped away.

Darkness feathered at the edges of my vision, when with a pop, I flung backward, free from Chuck's hold.

I landed with a thud on my ass, the fog in my head blurring in and out.

Blood coated my injured hand, more pouring out from the cut, dripping over the sides and onto the floor. I just stared at the ribbons of red, the deep punctures, my body slouching from sudden exhaustion.

Ava darted out of the room somewhere, while Bond swept me into his arms and carried me after my friend.

"She's lost too much blood," she stammered, then a flickering flame illuminated from a phone, revealing we stood in a filthy bathroom. Black grout filled the space between the tiles, the smell reminding me of a place locked up for too many years without ventilation.

"I-I'm fine." Still, the room swayed back and forth, and I gripped onto Bond's chest, admiring how handsome he was, how he hadn't shaved for days and I adored his rugged look.

Ava grasped my hand and ran water over it, the sting pulsing up my arm, but I felt too drunk to know if I sensed pain or if it lingered in my mind. My thoughts zoomed in and out.

Judas was there, and minutes later, Ava placed my bandaged arm over my stomach. Bond carried me back to the main room.

"Chuck," I managed to mumble. He sat on his heels on the ground, shoulders and head curled forward as he rubbed his head. When he looked up at me, blood smeared his mouth and cheeks.

Bond lay me on the couch. "Rest," he whispered in my ear, and as if my body obeyed his command, I let myself sink into the cushions, let my eyes shut. The softness of breath stroking my cheek lulled me into a relaxed state. And I let myself lay there, knowing too well I'd lost blood, and I'd be fine... but I needed time.

TIME SEEMED TO SLIP AWAY, and I couldn't tell how long I'd been lying on the couch when my head cleared. I pushed myself up to find everyone sitting around on the floor, several cans of soda all over the place, along with empty bags of chips.

"Got anything with blood in it?" I joked, and everyone's attention jolted toward me. They moved at the same time, rushing to my side, Chuck remained sitting, his eyes still slightly hazed over, which came from healing.

"You shouldn't have done that for me," he murmured.

I rolled my eyes. "Yeah, I did. And I'd do it again in a heartbeat."

"Yeah, and if she didn't, I'd make her," Ava added.

Judas sat next to me, his hand on my thigh. "You okay?"

"Yeah, I'll be fine, lucky my blood is strong."

I glanced at Chuck when I said that, watching for any sign of his wild taking him over again.

"We've been waiting for you, sleeping beauty," Bond muttered, and glanced back at Chuck. "He's been a bit out of it to tell us what exactly happened at the hearing."

I tried to still the tremors, tried to keep the fear from my voice. Tried to hold it all together as I started. "I had no idea. No idea the Council could be so...so cold. I went in there thinking this was a complete misunderstanding, that I had all the evidence I needed to clear it all up. I was prepared to stand there and give them the truth, that the video was doctored, and that they had Bond's sister drugged and in a compound. But I never got that chance. I was so stupid." I curled my hands into fists.

"It's okay." Judas slipped his hand over mine, warmth sank into my knuckles and slipped between my fingers.

"They never cared about the truth, never cared about anything. They waited until Dad and I stood before them, and then Thorin and Brylee stepped out of the shadows and into the light. It was an ambush, plain and simple and the worst of it was that my father knew."

I lifted my gaze then, meeting Chuck's. The beast crowded his eye, rage glinting like the edge of a blade in dark eyes.

"This piece of shit called *Judge* wanted one thing. He wanted Vlad taken by his henchmen, and he wanted my father to choose a side." I met their gazes, Judas, Bond, Nero...and then Ava. "They wanted him to decide where his allegiance lay; with the Ancient, or with the Supernatural Council."

"It's a coup." Nero eased back against the couch. "That's what this whole thing was all about? A fucking coup, and they used Mor to do it."

Silence filled the room.

"This so called *Judge*, turned on the Ancient, and said, *out with the old* before Slayer and his men attacked."

Moans echoed.

Are you aware of the consequences of these actions? The Judge's words haunted me. "I can't believe I was so blind. I can't believe I didn't see how any of this was connected. It was all there, from the attack at my birthday, to the diamonds. Thorin and Brylee were all over it, working with Slayer."

A low snarl rolled from Judas' chest, the hatred clear on the Wolves faces, their lips twisting with disgust.

"So, they were in on this from the beginning?" Judas barked.

"Not them. The Supernatural Council. They wanted the Ancient out, but they needed my Dad to make that happen."

"That explains why they're burning down the Ancient's monuments and temples." Nero shoved up from the couch and paced across the room. "They're starting riots to take the Ancients down."

"Exactly," I said. "They intended to push the Ancients aside, to change the laws that had always been in place to keep peace, and as much as I hate to think of it, the Ancient used me too."

They all stared at me. Pain cut through me. "Why else would I be made an Understudy? A role which hasn't been filled in centuries? He was using me, trying to desperately hold onto to the one person he thought could save him—my father."

I tried to smother the sting of betrayal as Bond growled. "They had it all planned out, didn't they? You never stood a chance."

"Don't blame Vlad," Chuck murmured and looked away. "He was trying to do what we've all done before. Survive."

Chuck was right. We've all fought and bit and unleashed a Witch storm like none other to survive, and in his position, I might've used anyone I needed to. He liked me. I had to believe that, underneath the betrayal was someone who cared. I had to believe that. "The question is, what do we do now?"

I swept my gaze across the room. Together, we were more than a team, we were family. I understood that now, clearer than I ever had before.

I'd always felt the need to take charge, to control the situation, help everyone else be damned of the consequences, and look where I'd ended up? I couldn't do this alone... I'd made that mistake already. This time it was different.

"I can't go off on my own anymore. I don't want to. Whatever we do from this moment on, we do it together. We make a plan *together*. We protect each other and survive *together*."

Eyebrows rose, they looked at each other in stunned horror.

"Okay, who are you and what have you done with our girlfriend?" Bond muttered.

But it was Judas who smiled, and nodded his head.

I'd made Judas a promise, and I intended to keep it.

"About time you came to your senses." Ava lunged into my arms, both of us thrown backward against the couch.

My Wolves were there too, climbing closer, embracing me and Ava, and Judas gave a small nod, a special knowing just for us.

Chuck was on his feet too. "Is this a free for all hug?"

Ava burst out laughing and untangled herself before rushing to his side. Her arms looped around his middle and he kissed the top of her head.

Nero grabbed the remote from a nearby table and flicked on the television. We all fell silent as if suddenly hypnotized by the screen... something other than focusing on our current shithole of a situation.

A burning mansion filled the screen. Twisted gutters, charred posts, crumbled walls. Nothing to salvage, in a raging inferno of amber and red.

The screen panned out to show firefighters battling the unstoppable blaze, but something felt wrong... it felt too *familiar*. I leaned forward as my stomach clenched.

My gaze locked the mailbox at the front of the home in the shape of a castle. My brain seized, momentum gripped me, dragging me to my feet. *"No...God, no!"*

"Shit Mor, isn't that your parents' home?" Ava gasped.

It was my home.

My home...*and my Mom.*

CHAPTER FIVE

BLAZING NIGHT

My steps were a blur as I stumbled forwards. I didn't think...didn't fucking *think*.

"*Mor!*" Judas roared. "Stop!"

I stilled, one hand on the doorframe. The burn of panic racing through my veins.

"We gotta think about this. It could be a trap." Judas' heavy steps came closer.

And yet in my head all I could see was the inferno consuming my home. I wrenched my gaze toward him, fear desperate to find an outlet. I wanted to scream at him, to lash out at anyone. I wanted to break my promise, and rush headlong into the flames. I wanted to do everything I could to save those I love.

"We need to think about this." Judas slid his hand over my arm, pulling me gently until I stared into his eyes. "If this is the Council, then they'll be expecting you to rush in."

"It is the Council, I know it."

"Then all the more reason for you to stay hidden. Let us go, they won't be expecting us. We'll be in and out before they even know."

"And if they are expecting you?" I lifted my gaze to his. "What then."

"Then we're not responsible for the ass kicking we'll unleash," Bond answered and stepped closer. "Trust us with this. I promise you, I'll take care of your family like they were my own. Just like you took care of mine."

I could do nothing but nod. Helplessness moved in as Judas pulled me close, kissed me and then slipped past to disappear through the door. Bond followed, pressing his lips to mine and leaving. I turned my head, meeting Nero's gaze. He pressed his phone in my hand. "Call us as soon as you find her."

"I promise, I'll call."

He just cupped my cheek and kissed me before he left with the others.

"I'm going too," Chuck murmured and headed for the door.

"Chuck, no. You almost died." Ava rushed forward.

"Almost." he gave her a weak smile. "Keep that kiss, I'll be back for it soon."

Tears spilled down her cheeks. He wanted to leave, already half out of the door. "This is my family, Ava. I can't stand by and watch when they need me."

Ava gave a slow nod, her eyes red-rimmed with tears as he slipped through the door and left us behind. I reached out, and her palm met mine. Together we stood at the doorway, listening to the snarl of the engine and then watched the blinding headlights as they backed out of the driveway and then drove away.

I'd never felt so lonely.

Never felt so helpless watching them rush headlong into danger. "This fucking sucks."

"Doesn't it just?" she murmured and then turned away.

Her hand slipped from mine as she returned to the TV.

But the news reports weren't done.

"This just in, Jessica. Authorities are saying three more fires have been started around the district. Two out in Blackthorne Forest, and one more at the Bestias Academy grounds..."

I spun, jerking my gaze to the screen as Ava shook her head. "No...no...no." Her eyes widened, hand rose. "What the Hell is going on?"

I fumbled with the phone, stabbing the buttons and then with a shaking hand pressed the handset to my ear.

The phone buzzed four times before it was picked up. "We heard," Nero spoke. I could hear the shell-shocked tone. "Judas is trying to get a hold of his family. But it looks like yours wasn't the only family the Council is coming for. We just passed a Nightclub for the Wolves, what's left of it anyway."

"Looks like tonight the supernatural community here in Tricks City is at war." The reporter looked into the camera and then shook her head.

"It's not just the Vampires, is it?" I didn't mean to say it out loud, didn't mean for Judas to snarl on the other side of the phone.

"We're starting to think the same," Nero answered. "We'll call as soon as we hear anything."

He hung up, leaving me in the silence and the horror. "There's nowhere safe. Not if this is bigger than us." I lifted my gaze to Ava. "There's nowhere we can run, nowhere we can hide. The Council will find us."

My best friend was still for a second, and then she lunged for her bag and dumped it on the couch with all the other items the Wolves carried from the cars.

"What is it?" My heart gave a clench as she speared her fingers inside the bag and searched.

"Come on...*come on!*" She grabbed her phone free, trembling fingers stabbing the buttons before she lifted the phone to her ear.

Her parents.

I took a step closer, drawn by the wide-eyed look of terror as the phone rang and rang.

"Come on, Momma," Ava whispered.

I looked at her, and then found the TV screen as there were more pictures of the fires, more clubs being razed to the ground...more evidence that the Council wasn't just after the Vampire community, but after *all* communities.

"She's not answering," Ava murmured. "She *always* answers."

I stepped closer as Ava yanked the phone away and pressed another button.

She tried to call. Still no one answered the phone, leaving her to stumble backwards and slump into the sofa. "No one's answering. That can't happen."

Tears rained down her cheeks. She made no move to swipe them away.

She was crumbling, shaking and closing in.

I was helpless to save her.

The screen on her phone brightened, and made a *chirp*.

Chuck, the caller ID flashed. "What is it?" Her hands trembled as she gripped the phone.

"*Your parents are safe.*" Chuck spoke softly.

I tried not to listen, tried to give them privacy.

"What do you mean? I can't reach them...*I can't reach any—*"

"*Ava...Ava listen to me,*" he growled.

She stilled, hand pressed to her ear.

Soft careful words spilled from the phone. I didn't need to eavesdrop. I could see his words across her face as she murmured. "You had my parents followed?"

More words, more soft spoken words. Still her tears flowed. "You did that? You did that for me?"

I stepped away, leaving her to talk in private and wandered through the rooms in this place. My mind raced, trying to fill in the blanks. Not just Vampires...and not just Wolves.

Was this the end?

Footsteps echoed. I turned and forced a smile as Ava wiped the tears from her cheek. "He had them followed, apparently once he fell in love he deemed it's necessary to take care of my family was well."

My heart seemed to swell inside my chest. I didn't know if I could love him any more than in this moment.

"So, they're safe?" I murmured and reached for her hands.

"Yes, scared but safe. There was a fire in my hometown, and they came after my father. But he managed to grab Mom before Chuck's protector moved in. They're hiding now, but they can't stay there forever."

My family.

Judas's family.

And now Ava's.

"We need to find a place that's safe, one big enough for all of us, and one we can defend."

"A goddamn fortress," Ava growled, her eyes glinting with purpose.

"Yes, a fortress," my breath raced, a memory tugged at my thoughts. "They'll never get in, not with fire...nor with guns."

I dropped her hand as an image flickered through my

mind. "I think I know where. But I need something. The Understudy book. I need that."

Ava gave a small shake of her head. "We packed up all your things. Balefire wanted your room cleared out. Chuck and I argued with him, demanding that he give you at least the rest of the term, but he was insistent."

My stomach clenched with the words. Seemed like he couldn't wait to be rid of me.

"So, we packed all that into boxes and stowed it in Chuck's cottage. There was no way they were kicking my Vampire out, not without a fight."

I shoved away the sting of betrayal. I expected more from Balefire, thought he'd give me at least a fighting chance. Looks like I was wrong. "I just need that book." I met her gaze.

Ava glanced at the doorway. "And you think there's some place mentioned in there where we can hide?"

"I remember something, one of the Ancient's old meeting houses. I just can't quite remember where it is."

"If we do this, then we're in and out. We get to the cottage and then we leave. We can't risk being seen."

I nodded. This I could do. *This I had to do.* The Wolves and Chuck were risking their lives for me, so I'd find somewhere us safe for us to hide. "Deal, in and out. No one will know we're there."

"Let's do this," she murmured and grabbed her bag.

I took one look around Chuck's place, and then moved to the wall. If I was going anyway, from this moment onwards, I was going in armed to the teeth. The Council almost killed me once, they'd not get a second chance.

Ava stilled, watching me as I grabbed a pistol and a crossbow from the floor.

"Mor..." my best friend started.

I met her gaze, letting all the fear and the pain trapped inside echo through my eyes. "They won't hurt me, not again."

She gave a slow nod. This was our reality now. We were pushed into a corner and our backs were against the wall. She grabbed a pistol from the wall and reached around to tuck it into the waistband of her jeans before grabbing two full magazines and shoving them beside the firearm.

This was what we'd come to. This was what they'd created. I followed Ava out of the front door to Chuck's secret hideaway and to the car the Wolves left behind.

We climbed in, barely making a sound before my best friend started the engine. I reached over and slipped my hand onto hers. "I love you."

She met my gaze, blue eyes sparkling. "I love you, too. You are my sister, my friend. But they are coming after our families, so we need to do what we have to now. We're no longer school girls. We fight, and we keep on fighting." She shoved the car into reverse and backed out of the driveway. "They have no idea what they've created. But they will...soon enough they will."

The night sky burned amber and red as we shot forward and wound through the streets of Tricks City. I gripped the door handle, passing the Wolf bar called *Bite*. People still milled around the pavement, staring at the blackened remnants. One male turned his head, meeting our gaze, the silver in his eyes shining bright.

This was so much bigger than us, so much bigger than my father.

So much bigger than me.

I hadn't taken much notice of where we were on our way in. Hadn't seen how we were in the more derelict part of the city, but now as we edged toward the pulsing heart with its nightclubs and its bars, I saw the city was in ruins.

Painful silence filled the car as we slowly drove past fire after fire. Screams echoed through the streets. Terrible, unmerciful screams filled with rage and helplessness.

Those sounds followed us, ringing in my head as Ava swung the car down a narrow dirt path until the headlights splashed against the mass of trees that held Bestias Academy in its grip.

White smoke billowed up into the darkened sky in the distance. The school had been burned, but not all of it. Just enough to set an example. Ava switched off the headlights and killed the engine. She stilled for a second, and then turned to me. "We stick together."

I gave a nod and then pushed the door wide, climbing free. The choking stench of smoke haunted us as we speared through familiar trees, making our way toward the school grounds. Bestias had been more than my second home. It'd been my new beginning, my real start in life. I'd waited a hundred years, wining and dining with parents, rubbing shoulders with the richest and most deadly of our kind, and Bestias was for me. The only thing I wanted. The only thing I'd begged for.

I lifted my hand and shoved through the thick brush.

The Council had taken this from me. They took everything, crushing my hopes and dreams under the heel of their boots.

Memories of the night came flooding back to me as I walked beside Ava. Dad's terror as he shoved me toward Chuck. *Take her! Keep Morwenna safe!*

He'd known what he was walking into, and he also knew there was no escaping them, no fighting, no pleading.

There was only a choice and the bloodbath of a generation waited.

The smoke grew thicker as we paused at the edge of the treeline and waited. Fire trucks were still there, firemen hosing down the main admin building.

"Shit," Ava murmured and stared at the mess that'd once been our school.

I thought of the pond out back, and the Lion man who'd crawled from the water after being spelled by Ava and Salome. I thought of the night of the dance, and how stunning Judas, Bond and Nero looked. I thought of the power that had raced through my body when Nesrin and the cat gang attacked me in the gymnasium.

I clenched my jaw and turned toward the cottage in the distance. They were my memories, they were my battles, and now this...this was my war. I reached out, and grasped Ava's hand in the dark. This was our war.

We took the first step together, holding hands as we hurried from the treeline and across the asphalt driveway to the grass. Hellhound guards patrolled the grounds, but they were sticking to the burned out building and the entrance to the dorms.

They weren't looking for two wayward misfits racing along the pavement toward the small cottage on the edge of the grounds. They weren't looking for me...

"There you are," a voice cut through the air. Shadows moved as Nesrin stepped out from behind the corner of the cottage. "I knew you'd turn up eventually."

Her white fangs shone in the dark. Black eyes sparkling like stars in the night as she took a step forward. Ava stopped, scanned the rest of the building and glanced toward the Hellhound guards heading this way.

"What the fuck are you doing, Nesrin?" Ava took a step closer and hissed.

"Waiting for you fuckers, what does it look like, Blondie?" She snarled and lifted her hand, checking her nails.

"What for?" I followed, keeping my voice low as I made for the gate at the side of the cottage.

"To fight of course," she answered, so matter of fact, and then lowered her hand. "I want in on whatever your hair-brained scheme is...and I want in now."

I shook my head, this wasn't the time nor the place for this shit. "Move out of the way."

She turned her head at the faint sound of footsteps heading our way. "I don't think so." The way she said it made my stomach clench. A smile followed in her lips as she crossed her arms across her chest and sucked in a breath.

I knew what was coming...we both did. Ava lunged toward her, half tackling the Panther to the ground in an effort to slap a hand over her mouth.

The result was a muffled giggle amongst a tangle of arms and legs.

"Oh," Nesrin called out under Ava's hand. "I haven't had this much action in like...*forever*."

"Shut it," Ava growled softly, and then jerked her head towards the guard as a call cracked through his two-way radio.

There was a soft snigger from Nesrin before the guard's footsteps sounded once more...only this time they were moving away.

Ava slid her hand slowly from Nesrin's lips, and the Panther looked up at me from the ground. "I want in. You know me, Mor. I won't give up. I'll be the biggest pain in the ass—"

"Fine," I answered.

"What?" Ava jerked her gaze to mine and then shoved from Nesrin with an *oof* from the Panther. "You can't be serious?"

"What do you want me to do? She wants in, and to be honest, we're going to need all the help we can get," I hissed. "Nesrin might be a bitch, but she's a fierce bitch."

"Thank you," she murmured. "So glad we finally see eye to eye on the matter."

"On one condition," I answered, stopping her.

"Go on." She shoved up from the ground.

"Every decision you make goes through all of us. You make so much as a sneeze without running it past me and we leave you behind. I'm not joking on this, you have no idea what we're up against here. One wrong move could be the death of those we love."

"You think I don't know that?" The cruel glint sparkled in her eyes as she took a step toward me. "They came after my little sister," she snarled, baring her teeth. "They tried to abduct her, tried to hurt her. My parents were there, thank the Ancient. But *no one messes with my family and lives. No one.*"

I saw her now, saw the hate and the terror burning her up like it was all of us.

She had as much at stake here as I did. "Then first things first, we need a place to hide, not just for us, for our families, and I know just the place. But I need to get in there, to find it." I lifted a hand and pointed at the darkened front windows of the cottage.

"Then what the Hellhound are you waiting for?" She growled and stepped out of the way. "Let's go find it."

CHAPTER SIX

HE'S GONE

The hinges squealed on the gate. All three of us stilled, glanced at each other and then pushed forward. "We need Huntleigh," I whispered. "She picked the lock the last time."

"Ah, I don't think we're going to need that," Ava murmured and then rushed forward.

The rear door was open, letting darkness in.

"*Jubba!*" Ava cried out and lunged for the open door.

Fear cut through my chest as I followed, pushing through.

"Jubba, honey. Come here," Ava called softly and moved through the darkened space.

I listened to her as she softly whispered, urging him forward with plea after plea. Nesrin even helped, looking in the darkened rooms with her perfect night vision before she stepped out of the bedroom. "He's not here. The scent is old, a day or two at least. I'm sorry, Ava, but he's gone."

My best friend slumped to the ground and lowered her head. Soft shudders cut through her body. I knelt down, pulling her toward me, and held her while she cried. "He's so little, he doesn't even know how to survive out there."

I closed my eyes taking in her agony and torment. "He will survive. I *know* he will. He'll learn to hide. He'll learn to run. He'll learn how to fight because he has no other choice. Look at me." I lifted her chin until her gaze met mine. Tears spilled down her cheeks. "He is just like us. We will survive this and so will he. We're going to leave out food and water and we'll come back all the time in case he returns."

"I can hunt him, if you want." Nesrin shifted from one foot to the other.

Ava just shook her head. "No, you'll scare him. He'll just run further away. We're all he knows, Mor. We're the only family he remembers."

"I know." I swallowed the lump in the back of my throat.

Honey badgers were tough little critters, but the thought of him out there alone...tears welled in my eyes and spilled free. "Come on. We'll get this book and then we're coming back to look for him, just you and me."

One nod of her head and she shoved her hand against the floor and pushed to stand. I scanned the darkness, moving to the empty stainless bowl. "You fill his bowl and I'll find the book."

Ava sniffed and swiped her hand across her nose. "It's in a box in the spare room."

I hurried into the darkened room, listening to Nesrin as she helped Ava. Taps howled, water splashed into a container as I searched the room, finding a stack of boxes in the corner.

It was here. I just knew it was. I yanked the container open and searched the contents. But there were just clothes, and shoes at the bottom. Clothes I once cared about...clothes I once thought were everything.

I shoved the box aside, letting it fall. The contents spilled across the floor, but I was already grabbing the next one, yanking open the top to spear my hand inside.

"We gotta go," Nesrin growled from the doorway. "Balefire's goons are headed this way."

I shook my head. I couldn't leave. Not yet. Not until I found the book.

"Did you hear me, *Vampire?*" I shoved the box aside and grabbed the next one as Nesrin shoved from the doorway and cut across the room to grab my arm and lean close to snarl. "We *have* to go. Now!"

"No." I met her gaze. "Not without *that* book. I can't..."

She shoved my arm away and then turned her gaze to the window. I could hear them out there. The heavy thud of their hearts, footsteps muffling the beat. There were at least three of them...three massive Hellhounds whose sole purpose was to hunt.

We were fucked.

Nesrin gave a snarl and took a step away. "You fucking owe me for this, Livingstone. Find the goddamn book. If you leave without me I swear I'm gonna piss all over your goddamn parade."

She was gone in an instant, bounding through the doorway and tearing along the hallway. I traced her footsteps all the way through the rear door and along the side.

"Fire!" she called through the night. "There's a fire in the boy's dorm. Oh *my God!*" Nesrin screamed. "Hurry! This way!"

The commotion was instant. Barking orders filled the night. Nesrin's shrill, panicked screams became louder and louder as the three Hellhounds took off after her.

I waited for a second and then hurried back to the room, tearing the next box from the stack and yanking it open. It was heavy...falling hard to one side as I pulled it down. I grabbed the side, and yanked the contents free, and the heavy Understudy journal flopped to the floor with a *thud*.

Hope surged through me as I heaved it from the floor and opened the pages. My fingers danced across the edges as I flicked through the book, searching for the darkened sketch.

I could faintly see it in my head, but the details were fuzzy.

"Mor," Ava whispered. "We have to go."

I jerked my head from the page and gave a nod as the pages turned and I saw what I was looking for. The charcoal sketch filled the page with a towering monolithic Goliath. "I've found it." I jerked my head upwards. "I found it."

"Then let's go," she urged. "Before Nesrin gets pissed off with us."

She was right. My chest fluttered, feet barely hitting the ground as I lunged toward her. Ava was fast, tearing through the cottage she'd once shared with Chuck and made for the rear door.

Shouts and screams cut through the air in the distance. I had no idea how Nesrin was planning on getting away, especially when Balefire's guards figured out there was no damn fire.

They'd be pissed. More than pissed, there'd be Hellfire to pay.

That thought drove me, slamming my boots into the pavement as we tore through the side gate of the cottage and across the pavement. We hit the tree line before we knew and careened through the thorny brushes and low hanging branches, designed to poke out a damn eye.

We ran like the Devil himself was after us, and we were probably right—although I was fairly sure even the Devil had nothing on Nesrin when she was filled with rage.

I stole a glance behind me catching a dark blur at the edge of my vision. It was fast, bounding through the trees, angling toward us. The creature's sleek midnight fur shone in the night. Wide eyes flicked toward me and then straight ahead. White fangs shone as the beast curled black lips and snarled, urging me to run faster. And faster I did. Clutching the massive book under one arm, I ducked and lunged over a fallen tree. The Panther took both in one giant leap to hit the ground hard.

Behind us came the thunder of pounding paws.

Hounds.

No. Hellhounds.

My insides clenched, I jerked my gaze to Ava as she surged ahead, spearing for the clump of Ash trees where we'd left the car.

The bays of Balefire's Hounds sent a panicked *thud* through my chest. We weren't going to make it...we weren't going to make it.

Thunderous paws beat the ground. The guards were bearing down on us, closing in. I tore past the first Ash tree as the car's engine came alive. Headlights burned through the branches, blinding me as I shot free and lunged. One hand grasped the door. I vaulted clean through the open window as that midnight beast lunged and hit the side.

But the Hounds were fast, and strong. Nesrin hit the side of the four wheel drive with a brutal *bang!* Claws raked the side, shredding steel with a piercing squeal.

Ava gunned the engine and flicked the high beams on. Terror was in the backseat as the Hound gripped Nesrin's rear leg and tore her free. I dropped the book, gripped the crossbow and rose on the seat, climbing until I shoved through the soft-top and aimed the weapon at the guard. *"Hey!"*

The flames of Hell burned in his eyes.

"I *will* fucking shoot you if you don't let her go *right the fuck now!"*

The Hound's midnight nostrils flared, but it stopped dragging her backwards. I aimed the weapon on the center of his chest, my finger slipping through the guard to rest on the trigger. I wasn't bluffing. Not in the fucking slightest.

And he knew it.

He released Nesrin, letting her limp toward the car. Claws raked the side of the vehicle as the Panther scrambled to pull herself inside the vehicle. Ava shoved the car in gear, but I never wavered, moving with the vehicle as we shot forward...until we were too far away for the infernal bastard to take a running leap and try his luck one more damn time.

Ava cut a panicked glance to Nesrin as she shoved between us, shifting back to human form and spilled into the backseat. She gave a moan and then a whimper. I sank into the seat, moving the crossbow to set it on the floor once more.

"Nesrin," I murmured and turned toward her.

"Don't *fucking talk to me,"* she snarled and grabbed her bare leg.

The fang marks were deep, leaving blood to ooze from the puncture wounds. Long strands of midnight hair lashed pale skin as she thrashed, bare as the day she was born.

"There's a jacket in the backseat." Ava took one glance over her shoulder and then turned back to the road, her cheeks growing red.

I reached further, shoving my hand to the floor behind the seat.

"I've got it," Nesrin growled and sucked in hard breaths. "Just don't fucking crash tentacle breath."

Ava's lips curled, and she muttered something under her breath that sounded like *"Only if I can wipe out the back seat."*

Nesrin found the long navy blue, weather-proof jacket and pulled it on, zipping it up just enough to cover the peaks of her breasts. *"Well?"* she snapped. "Did you get what you wanted? You better have, or Imma bite *you* in the ass."

"It was the leg," Ava muttered.

"What?" Nesrin growled and leaned closer, staring daggers at my best friend.

Ava glanced into the rear view mirror and repeated. "You were bit in the leg, not the ass."

"I know where the Hell I was bit. You think I don't know my leg from my ass?"

"I wasn't sure," Ava said carefully. "Sometimes it's hard for me to tell that from your face."

"My face?" Nesrin drawled. One brow arched higher, all of a sudden the bite was forgotten...*everything was forgotten.* "Did you just call me *ass face?"*

"If the ass fits,' Ava muttered.

I froze. Ava froze. Nesrin froze.

The silence was chilling, growing tentacles of its own to strangle us where we sat.

Until with a burst of laughter Nesrin reached out and slapped Ava's arm. "You are hilarious, Squid brain. Just...*don't eat me."*

"I have standards," Ava answered and headed the car toward the city.

Nesrin sat back against the seat, chuckling. I grabbed the book from the floor and flicked through the pages to the black sketch of the gigantic midnight palace. I skimmed through the elegant scrawl. *Anarchy Haven, birthplace of the Ancient following.*

"Anarchy Haven," I murmured and lifted my gaze to Ava.

"Sounds like the perfect place," she answered. "Where is it?"

I searched for an address, finding just a word written on the bottom of the page. *Freedom.* "I don't know."

"What?" Ava glanced in the rear view mirror and then turned, weaving the car into the back streets of Tricks City.

"I said, I don't know. All I have is a word, *Freedom.*"

"Freedom Hollow," Nesrin growled from the backseat and curled the jacket tighter around herself.

I jerked my gaze toward her and heaved the book higher, slamming my hand against the flapping pages. "You know where this is?"

She leaned forward, peered at the sketch before slumping back in the seat. "You mean the tower for the Ancients? Yeah, of course I do."

I stared at her waiting as she glanced at Ava, and then the burning city outside.

"*Well?*" Hell it was like trying to yank out her damn claws. "Are you going to tell us, or just leave us hanging?"

"*What?*" The harsh bark filled my head. "Don't tell me the good little Vampire Princess doesn't even know about the most dangerous temple that's ever been built."

Panic raced, filling my veins. "Tell me."

The smile slowly slipped from her lips. Fear moved in to sparkle like stars in her eyes. "Oh shit, you don't."

I ground my jaw, and tried to not let it get to me. I was

supposed to be the damn Understudy to the Ancient and how come I was only hearing about this Anarchy Haven now?

Nesrin glanced at Ava and then settled on me once more, only this time the cockiness was gone. "It's a place Dad told me to never go. A bad place. A *powerful place.*"

I jerked my gaze to Ava as she slowly drove through the City streets watching the streets behind us the rear view mirror. "Doesn't look like we have much of a choice though, does it?"

I waited for Nesrin to explain while Ava's words settled deep. She was right. We were running out of options. I lowered my gaze to the sketch in the Understudy. *Freedom.* The word burned inside my mind. It felt like all roads had led us here, to this moment, and this page.

Judas and the others were out there saving those we loved. We needed a place to hide them. A place to protect them. A place where the Supernatural Council might think twice before invading.

And this sounded like the perfect option. "I don't care, the address, Nesrin. Now."

"Fine," she gave a shrug. "Suit yourself. You know Hudson's corner. The nice end of the City, with the flash houses and fast cars?"

My heart sped. "Yeah?"

"Well, it's nowhere near that."

I wanted to punch her. Literally punch her. My lips curled, teeth bared as she gave a chuckle and then glanced to Ava. "Take a right, fish eyes, and follow that road all the way to the end."

Ava turned, blue eyes darkening like an oncoming storm. "If we have to decide the first person to be in the Council's firing line, I'm volunteering Nesrin."

"Oh, you're so sweet." The drawl was almost sickening from the backseat. "I didn't know you cared."

Fists strangled the wheel as Ava turned to the road ahead once more. I didn't need to be a damn psychic to know who she was strangling inside her mind.

"Fish eyes? Tentacle breath?" she muttered.

"Dad warned me for good reason." Nesrin had dropped the playful, let's rile Ava up demeanour. "I've heard some pretty bad things about that place. It's why it's condemned."

"And why wasn't it demolished then, if it's so bad?" I muttered, not really believing a word she said.

"Dad said they couldn't, said that when they sent a team to tear the place down, those people were never seen again. It's not just a temple, not just a place. It's a beast all of its own. A living, *breathing, hungry beast.*"

An icy touch raced along my spine. I shuddered and sat back in the seat, pulling the tome into my lap. Something about it didn't feel right. How could a place called Freedom be so deadly?

"See that alley." Nesrin leaned forward and pointed to a gap between two brick buildings. "Turn there."

Ava slowed the car and eased us into the narrow gap. I shifted my gaze to the side, mirror, taking one last look of the city we left behind. I'd not been in this part of the city. Not with my father, or on my own, and for some strange reason I wondered why?

Headlights splashed against the mossy green brickwork as we exited into another side street. Only it's a street that didn't run north-south. It was a street that disappeared in an arc. "This doesn't look right."

"It's a circle." Nesrin leaned forward, pushing her face against mine as she stared through the windscreen. "The circle of life...or death, depending on who you ask."

The buildings here were dark and lonely. There wasn't a bright colored door, not a pretty curtain draped in the window. There was only dark, cold stone.

Nesrin lifted her hand and pointed. "Keep following the road. You won't miss it."

Ava eased the car along the curved street, until she came to a dead stop in the middle of the road, directly opposite from where we'd driven in.

"Holy shit, no freaking way," Ava murmured, turning to stare at the towering midnight beast behind the eight foot construction barrier.

"Way," Nesrin growled and shoved forward to climb over the top of me.

I swear she shoved her ass in my face on purpose as she gripped the shredded door of the car and vaulted out in one smooth jump.

Ava eased her foot off the brake, and angled the four wheel drive alongside the curb. "I don't like this," she murmured, unable to take her eyes off the menacing stone giant.

"Neither do I." I closed the book and reached for the door handle. "But we don't have much choice."

CHAPTER SEVEN

ANARCHY AWAITS

I GRABBED THE STEEL BARRIER AND YANKED, MAKING the hole a little bigger, and squeezed through. Nesrin was already gone, slipping into the darkness. But I found her soon enough, standing at the towering doorway to the sanctuary itself.

She never turned her head as Ava stumbled in behind me, only wound her arms around that slicker and stared up at the door. I glanced at the barricades, and the torn plastic sheeting flapping in the wind, designed to keep people from looking in.

They didn't look like they'd been ripped in a desperate attempt to get inside, but rather by the weather...and time. There was always goddamn time.

"Well, can't stand out here looking like idiots forever," Nesrin muttered and took in a hard breath, before she climbed the first of five steps to reach the massive door.

I swallowed, gripped the Understudy journal in my hands and watched her.

"Wait," Ava started. She glanced at me and then Nesrin. "If we do this, then we do it together."

Nesrin's shoulders sank with the exhale as she spun. "Thank Lucifer, I thought you guys were gonna let me do this on my own."

"Never." Ava stepped, making her way to Nesrin's side.

I swapped the heavy book to my other arm and followed, taking the other side. The three of us stood on Anarchy's doorstep, and reached out, grasping each other's hand.

"Let's do this," Ava murmured and reached up to the massive black iron handle and turned.

The door opened seamlessly, swinging wide enough for us to pass through, yet we still stood on the threshold, unable to take that last step into the darkness.

Nesrin's grip tightened around mine, and a shudder raced from her hand and into mine. She was scared, *no, more like terrified.* I took the first step, leaving them behind and slipped my fingers from Nesrin's.

"Mor, *wait,*" Ava called behind me.

But it was too late, I was already inside, dragging the dust-choked air of a thousand years into my lungs. The floor gave a tremble, sending a vibration through my feet.

Like a greeting.

Or a warning.

But the feeling carried, bleeding through my legs and into my body, stilling when it reached my chest...*and the remnant of power.*

"It's okay," the words slipped free before I knew. As soon as I said them, I knew it felt right. "It's not going to hurt us."

Ava was next, stepping forward like a timid mouse venturing too far out in the open in desperate need for food. She stilled beside me, a small cry tearing from her lips as she jerked her gaze to the floor and shoved out her hands.

"It's okay." I turned to her, grasping her hand. "It's just...sensing you."

"How the Hell do you know that?" She jerked her wide-eyed, fear filled eyes to me.

I opened my mouth to answer. I didn't know...I didn't know how I understood any of this. I just knew. Like I knew what we needed to do next.

"Call Chuck." My chest tightened with the words. "I'll call the Wolves. Give them the directions, everyone needs to come here."

"You really think this place isn't going to swallow us alive?" Nesrin called from outside the front door.

"You decide for yourself, take a chance, Nesrin. Step inside," I answered as that vibration turned into a feathered brush against my mind.

I knew this place. I didn't know how I knew it, but I just did. I felt the walls and the floor. I felt the soul, even through the inch-thick dust and stale air.

Still Nesrin waited, until I slipped my hand from Ava's and held it out for her. "I'm right here. Take my hand."

She stepped then, crossing the divide and jerked her gaze around the darkened room, searching for the demon in the dark. Warmth swallowed my fingers, as she clutched my hand like it was a life raft and she was about to drown.

"See?" I murmured. "Everything's fine."

She cried out, stumbled away, dropping my grasp as the same vibration raced through her body. "It's okay." I lunged for her, grasping her hand as she spun, and stared at the floor. "It's just touching you, just seeing why you're here."

"It's going to kill us," she cried out and lunged for the door.

"No, *stop!*" I wrenched my hand upwards, stilling her as she stepped back across the doorway.

A deep snarl whispered through the air. Now *that* was a warning. Nesrin let out a whimper and looked around the darkened room.

"I need you to do exactly as I say," I murmured and looked to the shadows.

Nesrin gave a nod. "I die here and I'm coming back to haunt the fuck outta you, Vampire. *Just sayin'*"

She died here, and there was no coming back, not in corporeal form or a whisper in the damn wind. That, I knew to my bones. "I want you to turn, and take a slow step, let the vibration in. It wants to know you're not here to hurt it."

"*It?*" She forced through clenched teeth. "You speak about it like it is alive."

It was...maybe not now. Maybe this was just a remnant of the place it'd once been. But at one time it was a place of worship, a place where those who stood within its walls poured out their hate and their hurt...and their love. They filled the space with their love.

I lowered the walls inside me, whispered words thrown from the darkness of my mind to this place of sanctuary. *That's it, isn't it? They gave you their love...and their hate.* "I want you to tell it that you meant it no harm. I want you to tell it the reason why we're here and be honest, it'll know if you're lying."

She swallowed hard and the sound carried. "I...I ah, didn't mean to piss you off."

I winced at the choice of words, but I'd asked for honest. Me and my big mouth.

"We need to hide, we need protection." She wrenched those midnight eyes to mine. "*She* needs protection. I know the stories, know what they said about you. Know they said once people coming in here, they don't come out again. But we're here to ask you to make an exception."

Ava's mouth gaped open. "Ah, don't you think that's enough?"

But once Nesrin started she just never stopped. "You know about the fires, right? You know about the Council?"

That guttural snarl echoed through the foyer around us once more, only this time is was deeper and louder, like it was shaking off the shackles and scenting the true enemy.

"Yeah, you know them." Nesrin took a step, lowering her hand.

The more she talked the easier it became. "They wanted to tear you down, right? They wanted to destroy every inch of you, just like they're destroying every other temple out there. That's why we're here. We're asking you to help us...*to protect us*. We're asking you to open your doors to those we love. We can't fight a battle if our family is in danger." She met my gaze. "And we want to fight. With teeth and claws, with everything we have."

That savage, animal sound rippled through the air, and then with a gust of wind, the front door opened wider.

"That's a boy," Nesrin urged.

The air snarled.

"Or girl," the Panther stammered, eyes widening as she lifted a hand in defeat. "Girls are kickass too."

But the winds of change had found us, whipping around the foyer like the beast of Anarchy had come alive.

"Call Chuck," I murmured. "Tell him to come, to bring everyone."

Ava shoved her fingers into her pocket and dragged her phone free. "There's no reception...*or wait*. There it is. That's strange, I didn't have one bar a second ago, and now I have full service."

"Not strange at all," Nesrin murmured, the hint of a smile creeping across her lips.

I dug my fingers into my own pocket, yanking my phone free. Ava was right, full service. I pressed the buttons and listened for the phone to ring.

"We have her," Nero's voice cut through the handset. "Judas is with her now, she's a little burned and shaken, but she's okay."

"Oh thank, Lucifer." I closed my eyes and whispered a prayer. "And everyone else?"

"The servants were gone, it was just your Mom at home. But Mor, your home is gone, and by gone I mean no longer standing."

I rocked back on my heels as memories flooded through me. All the parties and the laughter, all the good times, not to mention my wardrobe. "It doesn't matter," I murmured. "None of it does. I'm going to get Nesrin to text you an address, I want you to be bring. Her here, bring everyone. The Blackthorne Wolves, *everyone*. We've found a sanctuary big enough to protect everyone."

"You have?" Nero sounded surprised.

"Didn't think we were just going to sit around and wait for you, did you?" I murmured and lifted my gaze to Nesrin and the Panther's words resounded. "With everyone under one roof we have a fighting chance. We let the Council come to us."

"I like it," he growled. I could hear his heavy footsteps.

"And Nero."

"Yeah?"

"Your Mom, and her sisters. I want them all to be here too."

There was silence for a second before his voice turned thick and husky. "Thank you, it means a lot."

"Nesrin is going to text you the address, send it to whoever you need." I looked around me to the towering entrance, big enough to be the entire dorm of Bestias. "This place is massive.'

I ended the call and turned to Nesrin. "Okay, let's get everyone here, and then we can make a plan to get my father and the Ancient back."

A vibration tore across the floorboards once more. I knew what this place wanted, knew what it was asking. So, I turned, and looked into the darkness. "Ava, you get everything you can from the car. I'm going to take a look around."

I left them there, pressing the tread of my boots into the pillow soft layer of dust and headed toward a towering entrance and the darkness waiting inside.

It's not going to hurt me. It's not going to eat me alive.

Shadows gave way to a murky darkness. The ends of long pews were revealed the closer I came. A bitter cold kissed the tips of my fingers as I reached out and touched the timber backs of the seats.

Fragments of a memory came back to me, and in the space I caught the faint cry of a child. High-pitched wail that turned into a squeal.

Hush, Morwenna, my father's voice whispered inside my head. *Can't you hear it, this place, it's alive and it's listening to you.*

My heart thundered as I took a step into the darkness, drawn by an echo of the past. Squeals pierced my ears, but they echoed inside me, the trauma trapped inside, and that was where it stayed.

Only it didn't...did it?

It was here, trapped in this place, just like it was in me. I stepped deeper into the darkness, skimming fingers across the pews. "You remember me, don't you?"

Flashes came faster now. Brightly lit candles. Chanting. Soft at first, until the sound bounced off the walls.

See Morwenna, they're singing...they're singing for you. You and the Ancient. Dad's words gripped me as I walked deeper into the darkness toward the altar. "You do know me, don't you?"

The frigid air whipped around me, like this place took a massive breath, and on the exhale I climbed the long line of marble stairs. Echoes of the past danced inside my head, and the sense of familiar came flooding back.

I'd run along these stairs. I'd sat and cried. I'd wailed, lashing my father with tiny fists. But he held me, arms wrapped around me, clutching me to the silence of his chest. *He's listening, can you hear that? He's listening to you, he cares for you, loves you almost as much as I love you. This is our purpose.* "This is our Haven."

My steps slowed as I neared the top. "I remember now. I had my ceremony here. First my birth, and then when I was five."

There were more times. Dad had brought me here on our own. Just the two of us. *Three if you count Anarchy.* He was right. It waited for us. I stilled at the top, at the towering marble altar. "You don't need to wait anymore now, do you?"

Silence, just a brush of cold against my arms.

Like a caress...

Like comfort.

Footsteps sounded below. "Mor!" Ava called out, wrenching me out of the past and into the present.

"I'm here," I hurried back down the stairs.

"They're here," she called out standing at the doorway.

My breath caught as I raced down the last stair and back along the pews. "Who's here?"

I caught the blue in her eyes as she lifted her head and met my gaze and answered. "Everyone."

CHAPTER EIGHT

UNLIKELY REUNION

My feet flew down the stone steps, and if I had a heart, it'd be slamming into the back of my throat.

Everyone?

Jitters swarmed me, and an excited gasp fell from my mouth as I rushed down. A sense of pride and confidence and achievement thrummed within me that I'd helped orchestrate this, bringing families together against the council. An army to show them we wouldn't bend. As a single fighter, I stood no chance, but as a team, we'd unite and show them.

Chatter reverberated against the dark slate walls, stained with dust and dirt from years of being closed up. But not anymore. We'd fill Anarchy with Vamps, Wolves, Witches, Kraken and others... everyone who stood against fear mongering and hatred.

Following the curve of the stairs, the entrance hall slid into view, and my dead heart gave a thump as I gasped aloud.

Bodies... dozens upon dozens poured into Anarchy, the temple doors wide open for those in need. Families, guards, children, grandparents... everyone needing shelter, ready to fight for our survival.

I felt it. The hum of the ground, the walls, the ceiling... Anarchy accepted them, collected them into its embrace.

Dad would be proud, but fury came at me in waves and threatened to consume me entirely. I loathed the Council, and my hands curled into fists, my nails digging into flesh. I wanted them dead for taking my dad when he should have been here with us.

Judas wove through the crowd below and embraced his mom, his face beaming. His dad was there... Looked like all the Blackthornes had arrived, and I couldn't be happier for him.

I scanned the heads, searching faces, but couldn't find Mom.

Nearby, Nero spoke with his mother, while Nesrin walked past, helping her silver-haired grandma. Bond was hugging an older man with sandy hair... his dad, no doubt.

Emptiness spilled into my heart as I watched each of them come together and thought of my dad, maybe locked up somewhere. I rushed down the rest of the steps, the first sliver of panic tightening my chest that Mom hadn't make it, that something had happened since they left the house.

I pushed into the crowd, gaze sweeping the masses, but most flowed out of my way as if sensing the dread consuming me. I hurried aimlessly, my brain turning into a pool of conflicting directions. When I turned, Judas stood in front of me, his expression pulled downward.

"Is everything all right?"

"Yeah." I didn't want to panic him when I was doing a good enough job for everyone. "Have you seen Chuck?" A trickle of sweat rolled down my spine.

He shook his head. "Hey, come over here, I want you say hi to my dad."

With his hand on mine, he swooped me around and I glanced up at an older version of Judas. We'd met before, but unlike last time, now he smiled. Both stood tall and had similar deep brows and short chins, but he didn't get his dad's pale brown eyes. A softness washed over the man's face when he smiled.

"Great to see you again, Mor."

"It's great to meet you again, Mr. Blackthorne."

Judas was smirking at me.

"My pack is here to fight, to get your father back. What they did to your family is unforgivable. The Council's gone too far, targeting every one of us now." The bridge of his nose creased, the cords in his neck tensing.

"Thank you for joining us."

He nodded before turning to the rest of his family, and Judas collected me into his arms, leaving a kiss on my nose. "Sorry, that was kind of awkward."

"Probably worse if it was my dad. He's the king of saying the most cringeworthy things around my friends."

I scanned the crowd.

"There's Chuck," Judas called out over the chatter, and I followed his pointed finger toward the entrance where more people shuffled inside. When my eyes landed on my mother near the guardian, I wanted to cry with excitement.

"Mom!" I nudged my way past people as they inched into Anarchy. Sliding between bodies, I kept moving onward.

She met my gaze and smiled from ear to ear, waving her hand in the air. Helena accompanied her, and Chuck nodded to acknowledge me.

When I burst free from the crowd, I rushed to Mom's side, and wrapped my arms around her.

"Oh, Mor," she cried, her body softening against me, and somehow she seemed smaller in my arms than the last time I'd seen her. She trembled against me. "It was terrifying. Everything's gone," she sobbed.

"None of those things matter, only your safety." I broke our hold and studied her and then a terrified Helena. "Are either of you hurt?"

They shook their heads. "We ran with only the clothes on our backs when we saw them coming toward our home."

"The tunnels under the house. You used them to escape?"

"Yes. Just as your dad instructed us to in emergencies. We ran until we came out in the safe zone and waited for Chuck."

I swallowed hard, my chest on fire at hearing my mom's voice quivering.

"Your father..." Her words trailed off and tears fell, her hands covered her face as she cried, her shoulders shaking.

My insides broke. I wasn't supposed to see my parents this way. They were the strong ones who kept me going, who made anything possible.

I collected her into my arms, needing to be the strong one now, no matter how much it felt like a blade shredded my soul. My world was crumbling away and where there had been light, only shadows shrouded.

But in my head, Dad's voice screamed. *You're strong, Morwenna. Never forget that.*

This was strength without power, and it tested me at every turn, but I'd been through so much, I wasn't failing now. Not ever again.

I looked back at Mom who stared at me with panda eyes

that made me smile. "I know it's scary, but we need to be strong, Mom. It's what Dad would have asked us to do."

She raised her head as Helena handed her a tissue from inside her sleeve. Mom wiped her tears and met me with a new, steely gaze. "You're right." Her hand fisted around the tissue. She gazed around the room with stained black walls, at the lofty ceiling. "I used to love coming here. There was always something peaceful about Anarchy. It's a good place to bring us all together. You did well, Morwenna."

Mom rarely gave compliments, so I collected that one and tucked it into my heart.

"Chuck!" Ava's panicked voice streamed across the room, and I spun on my heels to see her shoving her way toward us.

Mom turned to Helena. "Let's go and see who we can help."

"Mor." Ava's voice drowned in sorrow, and a glistening of cold sweat coated her brow.

"What's going on?" I moved toward her.

"My parents, they're not here." Her gaze shot to Chuck. "Did you hear from them?"

His eyebrows bunched up as he dug his hand into his pocket and pulled out his phone. "They should have called by now."

Ava pressed up against my side, and fear stole the color from her face. I slid my hand into hers.

Chuck dialed the number and pressed the cell to his ear, his lips pinched. I worried for Ava, her family, but I couldn't think the worst... wouldn't.

With a mumble, he jabbed the number and dialed again.

"Something's happened." Her tone sank like a stone.

"We don't know that. Maybe they're on their way," I suggested.

"Then why aren't they answering?" she snapped, desperation flaring.

"I don't know, but I'm sure we'll find out soon enough."

"Leave it to me," Chuck insisted. "I'll find them." He pushed into the crowd.

"What's going on?" Nero asked from behind me, and I turned to find my three Wolves standing there, looking gorgeous. Even when we faced a war, I couldn't ignore the somersaults my stomach performed in their presence.

"Everyone's here but my parents. The Panthers, Wolves, shifters of every kind, Vampires, but not my family."

Ava's words got me thinking... "Not everyone. No Hellhounds, and where are the Witches?"

She twisted around to face me, her eyes narrowing. "Hmm, I haven't seen any."

"Me either," Judas added while Bond and Nero shook their heads.

"Chuck said he'd called them. Called everyone. We need them if we plan to fight against the Council."

"Then we go and get them," Bond snarled. "We *make* them join us."

"My car's outside," Judas murmured. "If we go, this is the time to do it."

I nodded, a new surge of energy rising inside me, a readiness to build our side, to be prepared for when the council came. Because they would come for us.

"We tell our parents to collect everyone inside until we return," I stated, already picturing the traffic we'd fight in the city to get to Blood Moon Academy, but there were back streets to make our drive faster.

"Let's do this," Ava blurted. "If I sit here and wait for my parents to show, I'll wear a hole in the floorboards and they already creak like a damn rocking chair."

"Okay. Let's tell our families and meet out on the front steps in five," Nero instructed.

Without another word, we took off in different directions, Ava calling out after Chuck, as I searched for Mom.

It didn't take long before I stepped outside into the early morning hours where the cold wind curled around my legs.

"If only I squished the Council, it'd solve all our problems." Ava murmured.

"Wouldn't it just." Judas joined us.

"A flamethrower might help if we could hone in on just the Council," Bond exclaimed.

Nero sniggered. "One better. An earthquake to take each of their homes, their temples, everything they cherish."

"Okay, we need to get moving." I raced down the front stone steps, the front landscape an array of overgrown weeds, skeletal trees stripped bare of leaves, and overhead an inky darkness from the coming storm stole the morning sunlight.

Let it fucking storm, let it rain and put out burning homes around the city, let lightning strike down the asswiping Council.

I jumped into the front seat, Judas in the driver's, the rest of the gang in the back. Ava groaned, and I twisted around to see her battling the seatbelt in the middle, while Nero and Bond pulled aside as she tried to find her belt buckle.

Judas didn't wait. He shoved the key in and ignited the engine, which roared in response. We were off, me pressed into my seat from the speed, while Ava wailed.

Back there, she squished against Nero from the sharp corner Judas took and I smirked.

"You're sitting back here, being the jelly in this sandwich, on the return trip," she threatened, her gaze narrowing.

"Absolutely." My attention swept from Bond to Nero, both staring at me with intensity at the notion of me pressed in between them in a delicious sandwich. I winked and turned back around.

No one spoke as we raced down the hill, swerving left and right on our seats from Judas' speeding. In the city, it wasn't long before we hit traffic, and Judas did his best to swerve down side-streets, but no matter where we traveled, chaos reigned. People were everywhere, panic in full force.

Smoke choked the city, and control was lost. Police sirens pulsed down every street we passed. People ran about like the world had come to an end, some breaking into stores, others looting.

"Fuck." Nero expressed all our thoughts in that one word. We came to a sudden halt. I lurched forward then back in my seat before spotting the line of cops in black uniform with transparent shields, fighting a mob of protesting humans, carrying banners.

Dump the Supernatural.

No Monsters in Tricks.

Stop Protecting the Blasphemers.

I cringed at the hatred. "The Council managed to make humans hate all of us, including them."

"Do you blame the humans?" Bond muttered. "I'd be terrified too if someone was burning down my city and home."

"We're going to stop the fucking Council," I hissed through clenched teeth, loathing the ugliness that they were spreading. It had taken centuries for humans to finally accept our kind into their society, and these actions would demolish that hard work in less than a day.

The cops in front of us shouted instructions at the mob, and Judas slammed the car into reverse and got us out of there, taking another side street, then another, until I lost track of where we were.

Looting and rioting smeared the city. Fire swallowed buildings. Tricks had become a battleground. Reversing out of another dead-end street, we swerved onto another.

I gasped at the sight ahead of us.

Half a dozen council lunatics in their red hooded cloaks spread out in the lane. One of them hurled a spear at an already battered and bleeding Wolf who ran from them.

My heart soared and I cried out, my hand jutting towards Judas. "Stop!"

The weapon slammed into the animal, piercing the fur, driven into its side, throwing him off his feet. His whimpers were a blade to my heart. Already shifting back, fur vanished, limbs stretched, and he took his human form. A naked man bleeding to death.

Ava cried in the back, and I fiddled with my buckle to get out, help him.

Judas grabbed my arm. "You're not going anywhere."

I screamed as the weapon came down, ending the man's life. Stealing everything from him. I shuddered, rocking back and forth in my seat. "They can't do this, they can't." The tears fell and all I could picture was my dad laying on the ground, killed like he meant nothing. Like he was an animal whose life didn't matter.

But he meant everything to me. He was my fucking world.

Sobs wracked through me, ripping me to shreds. I cried for everything, for everyone, for the future.

When I finally lifted my face from my hands, we were speeding from the city. In the side mirror, Tricks burned while a storm crowded overhead... the Apocalypse readied to swallow the city. I felt sick to my stomach.

"We're going to kill them," Judas growled under his breath.

No one said a word, we just drove in silence, drowning in the sorrow suffocating us. We turned onto a familiar road flanked by enormous oaks, up ahead, the Blood Moon Academy rose into view.

My skin pricked with a sensation I knew too well... magic. I rubbed my arms and shifted in my seat uncomfortably. The closer we got, the heavier the pressure pushed down on my chest.

"I feel weird," Ava admitted, and the others grumbled.

"The school's protected by a wall of magic. They knew the council were coming for them too, they freaking knew and were ready."

Judas parked out the front. I unbuckled myself and jumped out before he cut the engine. The air rippled with energy, the hairs on my arms lifting.

Blood Moon Academy towered over us like a looming ghoul, shadows darkening the place despite the sun sitting over the horizon.

The place sat quiet... too freaking quiet.

"You think anyone's home," Ava asked, approaching the closed gates, but the moment she reached out to them, she was thrust backward as if someone shoved her.

I rushed forward, as did Bond, who caught her in his arms.

"Holy shit, it's protected by magic," she muttered.

"That's what I just said seconds ago."

Ava twisted toward me. "Yeah, but I've never felt anything like this. Anything this powerful."

"United power can be unbreakable," Nero murmured.

"So, how do we reach them?" Judas stepped forward, staring into the yard beyond the gate.

"With technology." I slid my hand into the pocket of my pants and plucked my phone. I scrolled through my phone list for someone's number who could help us.

"You won't reach anyone, and you're not getting in there." A smug voice came from around the corner of the building.

A thin girl with long brown hair drawn into a low pony-tail strolled along the front lawn toward us.

"Huntleigh," Judas startled. "What the hell are you doing here?"

"Funny how you always turn up at the right moment and are the last person I expect to see," I stated, remembering the last time she came to me, helping me when I hid from Slayer.

She shrugged, her lips pulling into a smirk. "You're welcome." Glancing over at Judas, she nodded a hello. "Hey, cousin."

Looking over at all of us, her gaze finished on me. "You won't find the witches in there."

"Where are they?" Ava demanded.

"Gone underground. And if you're smart, you'd do the same."

CHAPTER NINE

LIKE A HOLE...IN THE GROUND

UNDERGROUND? I TRIED TO UNDERSTAND. "YOU MEAN like a hole...in the ground?"

"Wait...what? They're *in a hole?*" Ava jerked her gaze toward me.

I just shrugged.

Huntleigh cut me look of exasperation and shook her head. "They're in a cave, hiding...and you know, you two kinda worry me sometimes—like all the time, really."

Ava and I cut each other a glance before I turned back to the Wolf. She dragged a knife out of the pocket of her pack and used the honed tip to pick clean her nails.

"Well, are you gonna tell us about this cave," Bond muttered. "Or are we gonna hold a seance and try to find it that way?"

There was a sigh, and then a shrug. "I can guide you, but I'm coming as well."

"Don't think you want to do that." Judas shook his head.

"Don't tell me what I want to do, Judas," Huntleigh snapped.

"Suit yourself," he mumbled, turned and walked away.

Huntleigh just stared after him. She had no idea. He wasn't being mean...but I guess she'd figure that out soon enough.

"After you," Nero muttered and motioned to the car.

Huntleigh stabbed the knife back into the sheath, mumbled under her breath and made for the open door. It was only when the car door opened that she stopped, and then lifted her head, and then turned to each of us.

"Which lap do I sit on?" She winked at Bond.

He never winked back, only stared at her blankly. I wasn't the jealous type. *Not normally.* "None. You can take the end seat."

Bond gave a twitch of his brows and a hint of a smile before he held out his hand toward me. There was a surge of satisfaction, of knowing that I was theirs and they were mine. Always.

Bond slid into the car and shifted his ass to the middle as Nero rounded the other side of the car. I waited, reaching for Judas as he passed. There was a touch, fingers entwining, until they slipped, the tips kissed, and then he was gone heading for the driver's seat while I stepped into the open door.

Bond's hands were around my waist, steadying me as I ducked my head and settled on his lap.

"You want to head to Cedar Falls and take a right about a mile in. I trust you can find your way that far?" Huntleigh slid in and yanked the door closed behind her.

Nero gripped my thighs, pulling my knees across his lap as Judas yanked the door closed and started the engine. I met his gaze in the rear view mirror and gave him a wink. Wolves were jealous creatures by nature.

But this was more than jealousy. This was fear.

Judas steered the car east, heading back out onto the

highway. We needed the Witches, we needed as many people as we could get. Smoke still billowed into the sky as the sun rose higher. The bitter stench in the air followed. The city was burning, pretty soon there'd be nothing but memories in their wake.

Maybe we were destined to be one of those memories? What then? A world filled with the worst of us? A chill worked its way along my spine as Judas punched the accelerator, threading us around the back streets of the city and out toward the mountains.

The Witches had gone to ground. So that only meant one thing; either they wanted no part of the war to come, or they were getting ready to fight a battle of their own.

Trees whipped past as we sped toward the trail Huntleigh suggested. I lowered my hand, and gripped Nero's, watching as the car slowly started to climb.

"Up there." Huntleigh leaned forward and pointed.

I glanced to a gap in the trees, an old wooden sign had long since fallen, leaving broken stumps behind. Judas slowed the car as he pulled into the dirt trail and winced as the skirting scraped against the potholes.

"Should've taken a bigger car," Bond muttered, earning a snarl from Judas.

But my focus wasn't on the bone-jarring thuds, or the grinding scrape of the car, it was of the towering mountain that rose in the distance. The peak stretching up and tapering like a finger pointing to the sky.

"There they are," Huntleigh murmured.

"Where? All I see are damn trees," Ava muttered.

I smiled, it was exactly what I was thinking. We were becoming more alike every damn day.

"They're up there," the Wolf answered and stared out of the window.

"Maybe we should've called them? Sent up a smoke signal." Ava leaned forward, peering at the top of the mountain through the windshield as three ravens took flight from the trees at our right and cut across the sky.

"They already know we're here." Huntleigh stared at the birds and then pointed to a trail in the distance. "Take that one. We won't get far, but there's a small parking lot where you can park this piece of junk."

Judas clenched his jaw and said nothing. It was easy to see why they'd never got along. But he did as she said, turning the car into the trail until we found an opening. Clouds gathered above us, etched with grey as we pulled up and climbed out.

I sent a silent plea for the storm to head for the city and extinguish all the burning fires the Council had left in their wake. The *slam* of car doors echoed behind me. Huntleigh was already moving, long legs swallowing the distance. She was born for this, the hunter, the survivalist.

But there was one thing that nagged me.

I hurried to catch up, matching her pace. "I think it's time you told me the truth, don't you?"

She cut me a glare. "Truth about what?"

"How you know so much about them. How you know exactly what I was walking into with Bond and his sister." I stole a glance behind me to the others.

Bond lifted his gaze, meeting mine before there was a flare of concern.

"Tell me," I demanded. "This time, leave nothing out. I've been honest with you, done everything you asked. All I'm asking is a little honesty in return."

"You won't like it, best you leave it be." That was all the answer I received from her.

She surged ahead, climbing harder the steeper the track

became. But I wasn't giving up that easy. I shoved my boots into the ground, climbing until my thighs tensed with the strain.

She didn't know me, didn't know the lengths I'd go to protect those I loved. Knowledge was a weapon, one I was learning to wield quite easily. "She was your lover, right?" I looked back to Bond, unsure if he wanted to us to talk about his sister.

Huntleigh's steps stuttered. She swallowed hard but kept on moving. I'd shaken her. I knew it.

"She must've meant a lot to you. I'm sorry you lost her to them."

"I didn't lose her," she snarled, jaw flexing. "They fucking took her from me."

"And they put her in one of those houses, the ones with the drugs? That's how you knew what to look for, the marking under her skin?"

She just gave a nod. She shoved forward, long legs striding, leaving me behind in an instant before she shoved into a run, leaving me staring at her like a goddamn heel. My steps slowed, and a breath later the rest of the group caught up to me.

Judas reached out, grasped my hand in his and we walked together.

"She doesn't talk about it," he murmured and watched her.

"Such a fucking idiot." I could've kicked myself.

"Don't be too hard on yourself. Huntleigh isn't the easiest person to deal with. You just gotta let her do her own thing in her own way."

I squeezed his hand and for the thousandth time I wondered how I got so damn lucky. All three Wolves were the most understanding, most humble men I'd ever met. My life changed the day I met them, in the most extraordinary way.

I lifted my gaze as Huntleigh disappeared around a jutting rock. I caught the scent of sweet jasmine and lilac on the wind.

"We're close," Bond growled behind us and surged forward.

Nero followed, and Judas dropped my hand to do the same. It took me a second to understand what they were doing, but then I understood.

They were protecting me.

We weren't sure where we stood with the Witches. For all we knew they could be working with the Council. Maybe this whole thing was a trap?

The thought slammed through me, making me lift my head...making me stumble forward. Ava lunged beside me, punching her heels into the soft ground. My feet slipped until I caught grip and hurled myself through the air, following the others.

"Judas!" I roared, fear thundering through my veins.

I lost sight of them around the rock, but we were gaining ground, finding the trail that etched along the cliff face.

The sweet scent grew stronger the closer we came. Black birds flew overhead, cawing at the darkening clouds like a warning. I caught sight of Nero, he stood at the line of shadows, I got closer, and then I saw Bond and Judas...and finally Huntleigh.

They all stared into the darkness, unmoving.

"What is it?" I searched the darkness, fists clenched, ready to fight.

Judas moved, stepping backwards as I came closer, Nero and Bond followed, each one parting the way for me.

Tagar Lutherian stood at the helm of the shadows. He

had his arms folded, dark eyes finding me as I stumbled closer.

"Tagar?" I muttered and glanced to the others.

"Morwenna."

I felt the power the closer I came. Heavy, like a blanket wrapping around me. My steps closed in. Ava's slowed even harder, pulling her behind me. I looked down, seeing only the ground, until the air shimmered an inch above the ground.

A spell.

Goosebumps raced as I took a step, moving past Judas and then the others. I could feel it weighing me down. The only thing I didn't know was why? "Friend or foe, Tagar?"

"You know, I was thinking the exact same thing." He uncrossed his arms.

I flinched. "You know me. You know what I stand for. It wasn't that long ago we stood next to each other in battle."

"You don't have to remind me, Mor. It wasn't that long ago I offered you protection."

I lifted my hand. "So why all this? Do you not trust us?"

"I don't trust anyone," he answered. "Not even myself."

Black birds called once more, only this time more urgent. Like it was warning us somehow.

"Why did you come, Mor?"

I flinched. If he'd came all this way, then he knew why. It looked like we were going to play a game. "You know why. They have my father, Tagar. The same man you tried to help before. All I'm asking is you help us again."

There was a sigh, and a shake of his head. "This is different, and you know it."

"No." I jerked my gaze to his. "That's the issue. *This isn't different.* The Council has been behind this thing from the very beginning. Their true purpose has been to take down the Ancient, and when that failed, then they came after my father...*then they came after me.*"

"And this affects me, how?"

I winced at the coldness in his voice. "It affects you, because *you know this isn't where it ends.*"

"It does for them." A voice echoed from a clump of trees in the distance.

A growl echoed from behind me as the male neared. He was a Council member that I knew, wearing an emblem around his neck I'd seen in the Council chambers.

But he wasn't here to fight. That I knew.

"What do you want?" Tagar muttered.

I smiled as the Council bitch stopped walking, confusion and a little fear settled in his eyes as he glanced down to his feet and then found Tagar once more. "I've come to make an offer on behalf of the Council."

My stomach tightened. I glanced to Judas.

"What kind of offer?" Tagar murmured.

"A seat on the Council." He never once took his eyes from the High Priest. "It's what your kind have wanted, what you've bled for...what you've fought for."

"All I have to do is?" Tagar took a step toward him.

"Side with us, of course." The piece of shit smiled at me when he answered.

Bond let out a snarl and tried to lunge. "I'll fucking give you a side you've never seen."

Tagar lifted a hand, stilling the Wolf.

He was thinking, eyes sparkling as he turned over the proposal in his head. I couldn't believe it. After all we'd been through, was he about to turn on me now?

CHAPTER TEN

EVERYTHING IS NEGOTIABLE

THERE WAS NO SOUND, JUST HEAVY BREATHING. AIR, thick enough to slice, suffocated me, and a drop of sweat slid down my spine. Everyone stood in silence, locked in a staring match. All eyes were on the enemy, but my heart pounded, waiting...waiting for the High Priest to make a decision that favored us, not the scum of this earth.

The Council needed to draw the Witches onto their side because they knew that with the coven came power and strength enough to weaken us. Same reason I was here to get them on our side.

Tagar, the High Priest of the Blood Moon Coven, lifted his chin, lips thin as paper, and his blue green eyes locked on the shorter man who showed no sign of nerves. Unlike me, who sweated nonstop, or maybe it was lack of wind. The air stilled around us like it waited for Tagar to make a decision too.

He cleared his throat. "So, you're willing to give us a voice and laws of our own and in exchange we stand with you and burn the old ways to the ground?"

Ava gasped beside me, and I clutched her hand in mine.

The council member's mouth split into a toothy grin as he gave a nod. An agreement that they were buying out the Witches. Offering them representation. A voice. To change their tainted image.

I sucked in a rushed breath. I wanted to scream and kick the guy all the way to the moon. His widening smile sickened me. The Council had already killed so many but that was just the beginning, wasn't it? My feet slipped forward, muscles tense, but a hand looped around my waist, holding me in place. Judas' lips were on my ears, whispering, "You can't."

Fuck, I knew that better than anyone, Dad ingrained it in me for years, but sharing space with a murderer had me trembling with fury.

The Wolf shifter murdered on the streets before our eyes punched through my thoughts. The Council were killers. Everyone on their side had blood on their hands, and the Witches would too if they took this deal.

Judas' arm held me tight, the warmth of his breath on my shoulder helped calm me. Of course he was right, this wasn't about me, but the High Priest deciding the fate of his coven.

"What will it be?" the negotiator bellowed, like somehow he stood over us, and we were nothing but the dirt he walked on.

That time Judas twitched against me, his breath racing, but he stayed back and waited.

Silence choked me.

"Give me a day to think about it," Tagar announced, swallowing a bit too loudly. Nerves finally getting the better of him.

My heart clenched, utterly heartbroken to hear the possibility in his voice that he might opt to side with the

Supernatural Council. I exchanged nervous glances with my Wolves.

Brow furrowing, the negotiator huffed his disappointment, and as much I wanted to rip that scowl off his face, my insides caved.

Tagar was giving this thought... considering the prospect of siding with the enemy for power. I wanted to scream that he couldn't. Not even a sliver of his thoughts should go in that direction.

"You can't do this," Ava cried out. "They'll go back on their words and slaughter you just like they plan to do to us."

"Shut your mouth, bitch." The words spewed from the council man's lips like venom, his dark eyes piercing right through Ava, filled with hatred. He loathed us, and if he could, he'd burn us all alive. He didn't care about us or the Witches. This was a deal to benefit them, nothing more.

The energy in the woods shifted, growing heavier, and Ava's skin shimmered with the knowing with the signs of her transformation. Nervous voices behind us murmured, and Judas flinched against me.

I shoved away from Judas and threw myself at Ava, clasping my arms around her, dragging her away from everyone, out of earshot.

"Ava, stop!"

She wriggled in my arms, her eyes glistening, her skin clammy. "They're killing everyone, and we're just standing here pretending to be nice while that fuckhead smirks. He knows, he knows the Council will kill the Witches too, you wait and see." She wiped away an angry tear from her cheek.

"Sometimes the fight can be resolved without claws and

teeth," I said, sounding more like Dad; I embraced every-thing he stood for right now.

"Yeah, well, I can get a hell of a lot accomplished with just tentacles." Her voice trembled, and I dragged her into my arms again, holding her tight. Fear sat on all of us, pressing us down. The walls around us seemed to close in.

"I need air," she muffled against my shoulder and I released her from my embrace as she inhaled deeply. "Maybe I can just kill him quickly." She half smirked, her words whisper quiet.

"No."

"Not even a bit?"

I was staring at her wordlessly when Bond stepped next to us, his hand on my lower back. "Everything okay?" he murmured.

I nodded. "Yeah, we're dandy."

Ava grumbled but shook her head. "If I see that jerk on the street, I'm tentacle slapping him across the city."

I laughed quietly, despite feeling like crap inside. "I'll hold you to that."

When we turned around and re-joined the group, every eye was on us, watching, curious what was going on. My gaze swept over to Tagar, and something different shifted across his face.

Sympathy. Concern. Realization fluttered behind his eyes as if a thousand thoughts passed his mind in a split second.

"Now that the dramatics are over," the Council bastard blurted, turning back to Tagar. "We can't extend you the liberty of a day to make a decision." The sternness in his voice left me shaking with fury.

I stared at Tagar again, imploring him to make the right decision, begging him with my gaze, while he managed to hold himself together, giving so little away from his stoic expression.

The air was so brittle, we could snap it.

"I said I need a day. This is not a decision to be made lightly, you must understand this. And so will the council." Tagar stood tall, and an air of electricity pricked my skin.

With a wrinkled nose, the Council man snorted a half laugh, half huff of disgust. "I'll deliver the news and return on first light for your answer."

The High Priest nodded once while council member pulled down on his jacket, stared at us all with a sneer, and then marched deeper into the woods, shadows swallowing him.

"We should have ripped him apart," Ava snarled, and no one seemed to disagree.

Except I was locked in my place with dread, frozen by Tagar's temporary indecision.

With the Council guy gone and everyone huddling closer again, Tagar glanced at Ava, the Wolves, and lastly his gaze settled on me.

"Gaining a voice in the council is something we've been fighting for our entire existence." Sorrow drained through his expression, his posture, and my heart sunk to hear the ache in his words.

"This isn't the same Council. How do you know they'll keep their word," I answered, my mind flashing with images of Dad being dragged away from me, the disbarring of the Ancient with a simple command. *Out with the old, in with the new.*

"They can't be trusted," I added.

"I know." He expelled a long breath, shadows crawling under his eyes. I saw the struggle on his face and prayed he'd do the right thing.

Finally, he cleared his throat so suddenly I flinched. He glanced over to the woods as if someone sat in the shadows, when a man in black with short spiked hair stepped out.

"Get the others ready," Tagar commanded, then swung his attention to me. "Now, where did you say this Anarchy place was?"

Ava gasped out loud, breaking into a cheer. An explosion of joy spread through me. "Thank you. This is... this is perfect." Judas embraced me from behind me, his breath no longer racing.

"At the end of the day," Tagar added. "I couldn't live with myself if I supported someone who endorsed the mindless killings of innocents."

"You had me terrified there for a moment," I murmured.

He laughed but the strain remained behind his voice. He'd chosen a side and that meant fighting, but he was on our side, and that mattered more than anything.

Bond stepped forward, his phone in hand. "Let me show you how to reach Anarchy on Maps."

I turned to the group. "Tagar, while you get ready and head to Anarchy, I want to go after Dad. And the Ancient. We'll meet you at the safe house."

"I know the compound where your dad is," Huntleigh piped in, sliding alongside Ava. "I can take you there."

"You know everything, don't you," I teased.

"Told you before," she mocked and rubbed her knuckles across her shirt, smirking.

"Yeah, so who's going to win this war?" Ava added, her eyebrow arching.

Huntleigh shrugged. "Fuck knows. But I'm betting on your team."

The High Priest stepped closer. "We're going to make our way to Anarchy. We'll see you there." When he spoke, his words came with confidence, knowing he'd made the right decision.

"We're making a small detour and will meet you there," I added. "Our parents will greet you."

"I've already let them know," Bond announced.

"Good."

Tagar stared at me like he might say something more, but he just turned and walked out of the room to prepare for their trip.

I couldn't stop my smile from spreading when I turned to my gang. "We have the Witches on our side. We're going to kick some serious ass."

"Hell yeah, we are," Ava muttered. "Now, let's go 'cause these woods are creepy." She glanced into the trees, shivering.

A sudden cold breeze curled around me, and we wasted no time leaving the woods to pile into Judas' sports car. Me in the back with my Wolves and Ava, Huntleigh in the front giving directions.

"I was worried there for a sec," Nero said, clasping my leg. Bond held onto my hip, one hand wrapped around my middle like a seatbelt.

"I swear if he said yes to the council, I was going to unleash my Kraken and bitch slap him into submission."

Everyone burst out laughing... a nervous laughter, because it had felt like an inferno was about to explode back there.

"So what's the plan once we get to your dad?" Judas glanced over his shoulder at me, worry deepening in his gorgeous eyes.

"We check out the compound, see how many guards there are, and come up with a plan. Unless Huntleigh has any further insight to share?"

"We could leap in there," she murmured, not looking back.

"Right, so we'll just grow wings then," Bond snapped. "Fantastic, brilliant idea. Let's do that."

"Don't need to get snarky, Wolf boy," she added. "There's a tower near the compound, it could be within jumping distance."

"Could be?" Nero asked.

That time she turned toward us. "We're Wolves, we can jump."

"I'm not a jumper," Ava blurted. "And from what I've seen, neither is Mor."

"Simple," she mocked. "We jump in and go open the door for you, while you wait out front."

"You make it sound so easy, cousin," Judas muttered. "Nothing's easy."

Huntleigh shrugged, dismissing him. She slouched in her seat as we drove down the quiet road. Everyone else fell into silence.

On the outskirts of the city, traffic poured out of Tricks.

"Left," Huntleigh called out, jutting her arm out to point at the street.

"Which left?" Judas stiffened, and the rest of us stared outside.

"The street we just passed?" I asked.

"Yes!" Huntleigh's voice was crammed with sarcasm.

"Then give me more warning next time," Judas grunted.

After a quick U-turn, we joined the traffic and soon turned off down the right turn. A place with open land, peppered by trees and various industrial buildings. Half an hour later, and Huntleigh tensed in her seat. "Slow down and kill the lights."

Bond's arms tensed around me while I scanned the side

of the road we passed. A bar, warehouses, one with two trucks parked on the curb. Everything was shut. Too early in the morning.

"Park over there." Huntleigh pointed to a warehouse's driveway, and Judas swung in, the sports car scraping underneath. Everyone cringed at the sound.

With the engine switched off, he glanced over to his cousin. "Where is it?" We all looked straight ahead at a huge square metal building.

"One block down and to the right. We head out on foot from here."

No one complained. We all climbed out, shut the doors quietly, and followed Huntleigh who crossed the road where the trees clustered together. With their shadow as our cloak, the six of us moved swiftly to the end of the block before swinging right.

"Stop here," she whispered and pointed to an oversized compound with spotlights and chain-link fences. No cars out front or signs of guards. The place looked like Fort Knox.

"Fuck, how are we meant to get in there?" Ava muttered.

"Fly." Huntleigh pointed to the lofty old water tower overlooking the compound.

"Oh, shit," I mumbled. "We'd need wings to jump that gap." There had to be another way.

CHAPTER ELEVEN

Cold crept its way along my spine. I looked up at the towering steel building and the ten foot gates that ran along the front and winced. Not just their height worried me, but the top was covered with razor wire. "We're never going to get inside."

"Never say never," Judas growled. "We're getting in there one way or another. I don't care if I have to tear the damn place apart to do it."

Pride flared with his words, as the other wolves stared at the metal giant. The compound was different from the others. There were no guards patrolling the gate, no way we could overpower and gain the upper hand. There was just a fortress.

"The mountain." Huntleigh pointed to the far side of the compound. "The ground will be higher, those trees over there will give us a vantage point to find a way in."

We all followed her gaze, finding towering pines along the other side.

"Better than standing here twiddling our damn thumbs," Ava murmured.

Huntleigh checked and adjusted her pack and slipped into the treeline.

We moved quietly, Huntleigh slipping away with every stride. I'd never met a woman more capable...and determined in my entire life. The Wolves let her get ahead. I kept pace behind them with Ava. She grabbed her phone, checked for messages and then slipped it into her pocket once more.

"Any news?" I reached for her hand.

The shake of her head was all the answer she had to give. Her parents were still out there, still on the run, or hiding with one of Chuck's squad.

"I don't like this, Mor. I don't like this at all," Ava whispered.

I didn't either. Not one part of it. But we were running out of options and right into a damn corner. The Council wanted the old ways gone, and they'd take down anyone who'd try to stop them. Even now I was still wanted for murder.

This *was* the only way for us. We had to rise up...no matter the cost.

And what if that cost was Dad's life? What if it was Ava's...or Judas'?

Or mine?

I swallowed hard and kept on walking. Let's hope it never came to that. The *snap* of a twig cut through the air at my right. I jerked my gaze to Judas and then to Huntleigh as she kept walking.

"Just a damn deer," she snarled.

Before she said the words a flash of brown peeked out from behind a clump of bushes. The animal lifted its head, sniffed the air with a twitch of a little black nose and turned wide dark eyes our way.

One flash of a tail and it was gone, bounding between the towering pines before it disappeared. We climbed, making a wide berth around the towering fence of the compound to stop around the far side.

Huntleigh was right. We were higher. The fence was a little shorter. I scanned the trees that grew close to the top of the barrier. From up there at least one of us could get over the razor wire without tearing ourselves to shreds.

Huntleigh stopped at the base of the thinnest tree and reached around her pack, slipping a water bottle from the side "This is the one."

Judas lifted his gaze, seized the tree up and down. It was the closest to the fence line; it was also the weakest. "It won't hold our weight."

"Sure it will, tubby." Huntleigh took a second swig and screwed the cap up tight. "It'll hold one of us, and one is all we need, right?"

He glanced toward the fence-line and then back to her. "You cheeky little bugger. You were never planning on getting us all over the fence, were you?"

"I'm lighter." She glanced my way. "No offense; stronger, more agile and I know exactly what's on the other side of this wall. I don't think any of you do. Just be ready at the damn gate when I get there."

"What's inside?" I stepped closer.

She never answered, just gripped the straps of her pack. "Death is over there...and it's coming for your father."

A faint snarl slipped over the fence-line. I stilled with the sound as that growl turned into a low moan. The others stilled and turned toward the sound.

"What the fuck was that?" Bond growled.

"That is the sound a Vampire makes when it's starved," Huntleigh murmured and drew a long blade from inside her pack. "It's nothing more than a ravenous beast."

"Vampire?" I cut a panicked gaze to Judas.

"Vampire," she repeated. "Not one you want to mess with either. They're stronger when they scent food...even their own kind."

Fear plunged deep as Huntleigh readied herself, placed the blade between her teeth and put one foot on the trunk of the tree.

"Be careful." I glanced toward the fence.

One nod and she was climbing, fingers finding marks in the trunk I couldn't see. She met the first branch, but it hung too low, and the further she went, the thinner the tree.

"Easy," Judas growled as the trunk swayed.

Still she held on. No other tree was as close. So, it had to be this one.

"If it snaps..." Nero muttered.

No one said a word...or dared to breathe. Huntleigh gripped the branch and held on while it dipped with her weight and with one tiny grunt, she lunged through the air.

I let out a gasp as she shoved over the top of the wall, and then disappeared.

Judas jerked his gaze toward me. Nero and Bond...and then Ava did the same. There was a second where we stood there stunned before we all turned together and the lunged toward the gate. Steps hurried, panicked as another savage moan came from the other side of the fence. Huntleigh was in there and we weren't yet. Lucifer knew what she was up against...all to save my dad.

We raced around the trees. Judas lunged over a fallen log, and wove in and out of the trees. We were like madmen, tearing through the forest.

A cry cut through the air inside the compound. We

stilled, breaths sawing in and out. It was Huntleigh's cry... I just knew it. The sound came again, panicked and piercing. Blackbirds fluttered from the pine trees and flew across the sky.

The Witches were here, if not in body, then they had eyes and ears everywhere. "Help her," I growled, and lifted my gaze.

Something dark plunged from the sky into the compound. The fluttering of wings followed, beating against the terror inside. And with a triumphant roar from Huntleigh, we shot forward.

We tracked her footsteps as the raven rose in the sky, all midnight and bloody. It was a race against not just the clock, but against survival. Bond raced ahead, slipping around the corner, Nero followed with Ava close behind.

I tore my gaze toward the compound and raced toward the gate, but there was nothing, no grind to say it was opening, no call from inside.

"Hunt?" Judas growled.

There was no answer. There was nothing...until a piercing squeal made me wince, and the gate opened. Just an inch, but it was enough. Judas stumbled forward and shoved, making the gap wider. We all crowded in, pushing and shoving through the gate to the compound inside.

But it wasn't a compound. Steel walls like girders cut across the grounds, the entrance not far in front of us. There was something about it, something that didn't look *right*.

"Fucking maze," Huntleigh gasped, slumping against the wall.

She was a mess, long scratches tore right through her pants, leaving her thighs bloody. Mud covered her face. Her arms were dirty and smeared with blood. She couldn't even stand, just lay with her back against the wall...her pack long gone. All she had was the blade in her hand. We'd only seen her minutes ago...minutes for her to look like this.

"What the Hell is in there?" Nero tore his gaze from her to the entrance.

She sucked in hard breaths and shook her head. "You don't want to fucking know."

Ravens circled the sky above us, like buzzards ready for a meal.

"He's in there, right?" I turned to Huntleigh.

She gave a weak nod. "Oh yeah he's in there. I caught sight of him, tried to call out to him, but he was gone, kicking and fighting like a mad man."

Agony cut across my chest. I jerked my head toward the entrance. "I want you all to stay here. I'm not going to ask you to risk your life to save my father."

"You're not asking. We're telling you." Nero stepped closer. "This is bigger than you saving your dad. This is *us* saving our future."

They all looked at me with the truth in their eyes.

"If you're going...then you're gonna need this." Huntleigh lifted her knife into the air.

I looked at the others, one by one they gave a nod, slowly I stepped forward and took the weapon.

"Swing hard," she muttered. "And don't fucking stop."

Growls of hunger slipped out of the entrance of the maze. I gripped the blade and swallowed. "Then I'm going in first."

The world seemed to spin as I took the first steps toward the opening. A blur of darkness swept across the entrance. In a blink it was gone.

"We're right behind you." Bond stepped closer.

I lifted the knife and stepped inside. A shadow raced toward me, for a second I didn't understand what it was, until out of the darkness came fangs. I swung, listening to the gruesome *squelch* before a head rolled and hit the ground with a *thud*. The emaciated body toppled minutes later, falling in a heap amongst all the other grey, lifeless, skeletal remains.

Bond yanked his hand to his mouth and gagged.

The sight was awful, and the smell was worse. I swallowed the acid in the back of my throat as I yanked the blade back and stepped further inside, slipping around the corners and working my way toward the center.

There were bodies everywhere. Some crawled forward, hissing and gnashing broken fangs. Bond took the blade from my hand and stepped up to them, slicing the air, heads rolling in his wake.

He took the front, hacking and cleaving. We battled Vampire after Vampire and stumbled over the already dead before we came to the middle. But Dad wasn't here. He wasn't anywhere.

I spun, staring at body after body, some piled high in the corner and felt panic close in. "He's not here."

"He has to be, Huntleigh saw him." Judas shook his head and scanned the space.

Ravens circled the skies. I envied their vantage point. From up there they'd see everything. One bird swooped low, diving before it turned and shot straight up into the air and started circling once more.

"I think it's trying to tell us something." Nero lifted his gaze.

The bird dove once more, in the exact same spot. I lunged forward, tearing through to the other side of the maze. I searched for him while Bond hacked and cleaved and Nero and Judas lunged through the air, meeting the hungry beasts head on.

Until I caught sight of him.

Dad has his back to me, hands waving frantically in the air. Blood smeared over his torn shirt. He looked like he'd battled a thousand wolves.

"*Dad!*" I roared and lunged forward.

But he never heard me only slapped the air, warding off a ghost. There was no one there. No one I saw.

"*Daddy!*" I screamed as out of the corner came a pale, emaciated beast.

The savage hiss filled the air, its moan carried.

Judas raised the blood splattered blade, ready to hack and cleave as the starving skeletal thing raced forward. Dark eyes held mine. But it wasn't hunger I saw...it was fear.

"Judas *stop!*" I screamed as the Ancient Vlad Vasile stumbled forward and collapsed into Judas's arms.

Dad spun at the sound. His mouth was open, fangs bloody and ready to rip and tear. He was still riding the killing edge, still fighting to survive.

I lifted my hand, stilling everyone where they stood. "Dad it's me...it's Morwenna."

He just sucked in hard breaths, hands fisted at his side, until in a blink the hard, savage look in his eyes shifted. "Mor? Is that really you?"

Tears blurred my gaze. "Yes, Dad. It's me. It's your daughter, and I've come to rescue you."

CHAPTER TWELVE

RACE AGAINST TIME

"Mom's safe at Anarchy." I leaned forward from the back seat of Judas' sports car, reaching for Dad's shoulder. Somehow he felt softer, weaker under my touch. Except he was my dad, a powerful Master Vampire, and had always been anything but weak.

"Everyone else is there too," Huntleigh piped in.

"Including the witches," Ava added. "They should be on their way there. I swear I sweated a bucket when that Council asshole made Tagar that offer."

Dad's attention shifted to Ava, eyebrow rising.

"They offered the High Priest a place on the council," I began.

Dad huffed. "A tempting decision for Tagar I'm sure."

I nodded. "But he chose the right side in the end. Anyway, everyone's waiting for us at Anarchy," I murmured. "So many of the shifter packs are already there, ready to fight."

Dad's hand stretched up and settled over mine. "You found a way to keep everyone safe. I knew you would." He didn't need to say it, but the gleam in his eyes had my chest tightening with pride. We'd butted heads in the past, but there was nothing more rewarding than having him look at me like I meant the world to him, like I'd done something he approved of.

When he broke into a raspy cough that sounded painful, I slipped back into my seat, sandwiched between Ava and Huntleigh. My stomach sank each time I pictured the terrifying concrete maze he'd been trapped in, the putrid, the coldness, the terror. The Council tossed him and Vasile in there like animals. My blood boiled, and I hated the Council with every ounce of my being.

I glanced over my shoulder through the back window. Bond followed us closely in the stolen SUV. The Ancient and Nero were with him, while the rest of us squished in here, rather than travel with Vasile. I couldn't blame them since he... Well, he didn't hold back if he had an opinion, plus no one wanted to share the car with an old vampire who may not have eaten in a while.

Judas' phone gave one short, sharp ding and he plucked it out of his pocket before staring at the message. "Fuck." He handed the phone to my dad, who mumbled under his breath before passing it to the back of the car.

"We need to go faster," Dad ordered. "Now!"

I reached over and took the phone from Dad when Judas suddenly hit the gas pedal. We were all thrown backward into our seats from the speed, my stomach lurching.

"What the Hell's going on?" Ava jutted an arm up, grasping the handle above the door.

My gaze fell to the message from Judas' father.

Anarchy is under attack!

My stomach dropped right through me, and the world spun.

"What is it?" Ava leaned over and snatched the phone from my hand. "Oh, shit!"

"Message Nero," Judas instructed, and Ava typed the message with her thumbs.

"Drive faster," Huntleigh exclaimed.

Judas grumbled. "What do you think I'm doing?"

Dad shifted in his seat, the air thickening with tension.

Panic grew in my legs and stomach, an urgency banging inside my head like a tribal drum. I gripped the door-handle, my knuckles turning white.

"Anarchy will help," Dad muttered, but walls could only hold out the enemy for so long. All I could see were the faces women and children pouring into the temple.

"My dad will know what to do until we arrive," Judas stated confidently, but I heard the fear underlying his words.

Ava shuffled in her seat and took my hand. Her eyes glistened, and I squeezed her grip. "Chuck will find your parents," I murmured, and the whole car fell deadly silent. The tension built around us like a scorching furnace, and it nipped at my flesh, reminding me over and over that we might be too late. That we'd find everyone defeated... killed.

Fear beat inside me while my muscles tensed with the urgency to run, to do something other than sit here.

My knees bounced until Huntleigh placed a hand on one. She looked at me knowingly. "Calm down."

I frowned, but nodded. She was right... panic wasn't going to help anyone. Pushing back into my seat, I stared outside to the cars leaving the city, while we gunned it like lunatics to reach Anarchy on the other side.

Chaos rained down in Tricks, and I watched as the houses and stores turned into a blur as we passed them. I closed my eyes and felt the ups and downs, the bumps in the road, and I couldn't imagine what lay in store for us when we'd finally arrive.

The heavy clotting stench of fire slithered into the car, stinging my nostrils. Judas fiddled with the controls, hitting the air conditioner.

Ava pressed a sleeve to her nose, staring out into the morning where it should have been bright and sunny, except a cloud of smoke from the fires hung over the city like an ominous beast.

Far to our right, a fire still burned, black smoke curling upward, the golden blaze licking the sky, reaching higher and higher.

"They're not stopping until the whole city's burned down," Ava murmured.

"That's their intention," Dad confirmed. "Flatten everything and rebuild with their mark. Doesn't matter how many humans die."

My hands fisted. How was this any different from other dictators who eliminated thousands of people for their own power? My anger burned amber hot, pushing against me at the whole shitty injustice of everything. I didn't give a shit about power, only those caught in the fire, whether by accident or purpose, it shattered me to pieces.

"We'll end them," I growled. "They're nothing more than bullies."

Everyone nodded, but they were too busy looking at the chaotic city, burned down buildings, people still running down the streets carrying merchandise they'd looted. We slowed down, caught in the tail-end of traffic.

Edging forward, I stared out the front to see cop lights throbbing in the distance. Judas didn't wait, but spun the steering wheel, racing down the opposite side of the lane before swinging down a wide alley, sending me right into

Ava, my arms grasping for the seat in front of me to catch myself.

"Hey, watch those turns," she blurted.

"Sorry." I straightened myself.

"I'll always catch you, babe." She winked before returning to her staring match with the city outside. Stores remained shut, windows broken, one car we passed was nothing more than a burned husk.

Judas turned sharply, his hands slapping the steering wheel in haste, our back wheels skidding sideways.

Dad gripped the door handle, all of us holding on until we came to a stop, inches from hitting a car parked across the road in front of us.

"Fucking great," Huntleigh snarled.

I looked behind us to see Bond keeping a safe distance. Judas turned his car and slowly maneuvered us around the dumped sedan, squeezing between it and a fire hydrant.

Bond followed suit and it wasn't long before we cruised down a long lane. Everything was quiet as hell in this part of the city, like everyone had abandoned the location.

"Is this what being in the apocalypse feels like?" Ava asked. "We had those zombie-looking Vamps in the prison, and now it feels like we're the last people on Earth."

A haze drifted across our path, blurring a sun turned blood-red behind the curtain of fiery smoke.

"It doesn't smell bad enough to be the apocalypse," Huntleigh murmured. "There's no rotting corpses."

I cut her a stare, not wanting that experience in a million years.

"Are you now the expert on the apocalypse too?" Ava muttered.

Huntleigh shrugged, half grinning like she loved proving Ava wrong. "It's common sense. Everyone knows if the end came, dead bodies would be everywhere and they'd reek. Then diseases would spread. Plus, if this was the real deal, spreading across the globe, I'd be long gone and no one would find me again. The only way to survive."

Ava scrunched up her nose. "Then why bother coming with us now? This isn't a kindergarten party. We're fighting for our lives. Mor's risking everything, and I'll fight to the end for her." Ava's voice darkened, and I couldn't love her more than I did right then. We exchanged a quick look, a small smile, enough to know we felt exactly the same.

Huntleigh slouched in her seat, arms folded over her chest. "I know a worthy fight when I see it," was all she said, and we fell back into the silent bubble that encased us. Judas fought to find clear streets and lanes for us to make it across the city.

Ava was on her phone, sending messages, lots of them. Several minutes later she looked up at me, her face white as milk. "No one's answering from Anarchy. Nero said his parents aren't responding either."

Sitting tense in my seat, I trembled and hoped we weren't too late. *Please don't let it be too late.* An excruciating hour later, we'd burst out of the chaos and onto a road, also filled with traffic.

"We need to go faster." Panic swallowed my voice.

Judas swung the car onto the edge of the road reserved for cyclists or breakdowns, and he hit the gas pedal, the car shuddering from the sudden motion. Bond stayed close behind us, and I sat on the edge of my seat. When we turned down a side road, we kept going, and I sat back, closing my eyes, unable to look outside, to keep feeling like we were still so far away. Ava took my hand in hers and we stayed that way until we finally came to a sudden and abrupt stop.

My eyes flipped open, and Judas was already out, his door shutting, Dad too.

Ava scrambled out, and I rushed after her. My legs exploded with violent motion as I ran toward Anarchy. It lurched over the landscape like a goliath. Black and intimidating most days, but not today... today it sat quietly, doors shut, holding onto its secret. I raced across the long yard and rushed up the front steps.

Footsteps pounded the stairs behind me. At the landing, I shoved a hand to the door, and at my touch, the hinges gave a groan as one door opened of its own accord.

I squeezed through the sliver of a gap, darting inside, blinking hard, trying to see through the darkness. But already my chest ached and knees trembled.

No one was here, greeting us. When we'd left, bodies had crammed this entry hall... now the place lay empty and barren. Terror clung to my ribs, strangling me.

My eyes pierced the dim light, finding a single sandal on its side near the corner. Near the enormous pillar lay a handbag, opened, contents strewn on the ground. An old vase sat shattered at the back of the room, and only when the door behind me opened wider, allowing more light into the room did I see the splatter of blood across the once white flooring. The scuffing on the marble floor, the crimson smudges on the walls. A battle had taken place here... but I could barely see straight as the room tilted beneath me.

Ava was at my side, gasping. "Fuck, we're too late?" she squeaked.

"There's not enough blood," I stammered, hope curling around my mind. "Not for the amount of people in here."

Still, tears pricked my eyes as I ran into the adjoining room, the next and the next. My heels hitting the hard floor, my thoughts spiraling out of control.

All empty.

Turning back around, I met Dad's terrified gaze. "They're gone. All gone." My legs wobbled beneath me, shook me, and I stumbled into a wall to hold myself upright. "Gone! How can this be?" Had I made a mistake leaving them behind? I should have stayed, should have fucking stayed.

The rest of the gang stood there, staring at me for answers, but I had nothing, so I moved toward the man I'd always looked up to.

"Dad? What do..." I swallowed hard. "What did the Council do?" My dead heart gave a thump, and my stomach clenched. "Where is everyone?"

His mouth opened, but instead, the floor shivered beneath my feet. Was it warning us?

A rumbling sounded from deeper in the building, loud and thunderous like an army rushed toward us.

Panic sliced my insides, and all of us shot together in a tight circle, our backs to each other, while we waited, watched.

The walls shook, and the hairs on my arms stood on end.

"What the fuck is that?"

CHAPTER THIRTEEN

TENSIONS GALORE

"Easy," Dad muttered. "It's just scared."

"*It's scared?*" Ava stared wide-eyed at the walls. "I'm about to soil myself."

He just looked at her, gave a small, soft smile and stumbled forward. He winced when he walked, limping to one side. The sight was a punch to my chest. Lucifer only knew what he'd battled in that compound.

I turned my head and glanced toward the Ancient. He was pale and shaking, standing separate from everyone else.

"You know us, old friend," Dad called out and lifted his hand.

A whisper of something cut across the air, darkness and hunger sending goosebumps along my arms. Dad stumbled forward as the faint call of *help* slipped free from nowhere.

"You wouldn't have hurt them," he said like he read words on the walls. "Did you save them? Is that it? Did you protect them?"

And the darkness seemed to reach up through the wooden floorboards and answer. *Yes.*

A *creak* came from further back in the chapel. I turned

at the sound and Ava gave a little whimper. Footsteps sounded before Mom cried out. *"Dante!"*

We turned as those we loved rushed forward, spilling out of a darkened room. Terror and exhaustion on every face as our loved ones swarmed us.

Chuck rushed forward, heading straight for Ava and swept her up into his arms before he made for Dad. "Dante. So glad you're safe."

"Me too, my old friend." Dad reached out and grasped his hand as Chuck's phone gave a *beep*.

He reached into his pocket and yanked his cell free, one glance at the screen and he turned to Ava. "Your family are safe. They're not far from us."

"Oh, thank God." Ava sighed and gripped him tighter.

"Looks like we're a little late to the party." I turned at the sound as Tagar Lutherian climbed the steps of the Gothic chapel and stepped through the open door.

The entire coven climbed the steps and spilled into the foyer behind him. All thirty-something Witches.

"Not late at all," Dad murmured and stepped toward the High Priest as Mom slid under Dad's arm and hugged him close.

He stepped toward Tagar and extended his hand. "I appreciate you taking a stand. This war is bigger than the Vampires, and it's about time everyone else knew that."

There was a *beep,* and Judas grabbed his phone. Confusion flared across his gaze before sadness took its place. "I think they're starting to figure that out." He lifted his head, but it wasn't me he searched for, it was Dad. "The Council has just attacked the Blackthorne forest, they're burning it to the ground."

"Marcus?" Vlad murmured and stumped forward. "Is he...is he alive?"

The Lycan Ancient had been in hiding ever since the first attack on his temples.

"He's alive. But they won't say where. They've taken more than the forest and the temples from us, they've taken our trust."

"They won't win," the words slipped from my lips. "Even if we fail here. They'll *never* win. While there's someone to rise up and speak the truth they *cannot* win."

Vlad turned to me, his pale lips curling into a smile. Something twinkled in the darkness of his eyes. Pride maybe. I wasn't sure. But as I turned toward Dad, I saw the same glint, like stars across a skyline of eyes of every color.

"That's my girl." Dad beamed and hugged mom.

"Our girl," Mom corrected.

Dad just smiled at her.

Tires squealed outside, before a *boom* that shuddered the towering fence surrounding Anarchy. The heavy *thud* of a car door followed before a woman screamed. "You in there! You murdering Vampire *bitch!*"

I flinched at the word. All of us turned toward the doorway. My stomach clenched tight. I didn't need a damn psychic to know who she was calling...*me*.

I followed Judas and the Wolves as they cut through the crowd of Witches.

A black SUV had mounted the sidewalk and crashed into the steel barrier. The rear door of the car was still open. A woman stood in the distance. She was haggard, wiry knotted hair and black streaky kohl lined eyes. At first, I didn't recognize her, until she stumbled forward clutching a knee-length black coat in front of her.

Bond let out a moan, and then shook his head. "This is not fucking happening."

I saw her then. Saw the sparkling SUV, and the way she

stumbled toward the door, her terrified gaze gravitating toward me. It was her. The Commissioner's wife.

The dead Commissioner's wife.

I stepped forward, leaving the others behind. "It's okay." I lifted my hand toward her, catching the tremble as she clutched the coat tighter. "I'm right here. I'm not going to hurt you."

"It's okay? *It's OKAY?*" she screamed and stumbled closer to the first steps of the chapel. "You killed my *husband*. Murdered him like he was *NOTHING!* He was someone to me. He was *everything* to me...and I can't live without him. I *won't live without him*...and now neither will you."

She dropped her hands, and the unbuttoned jacket fluttered open. Terrified cries filled the air around me. Judas and Nero stumbled backwards, reaching for me as they went. All I saw were wires amongst the vest of C_4 strapped to her chest.

She held something in her hand, a button with wires.

"Lucifer's sake, she's going to kill us all," Bond muttered.

Everyone lunged back into Anarchy as panicked thoughts filled my head. Maybe the walls of this place could withstand the blast...and maybe they couldn't. Either way there'd be casualties.

Movement came from the corner of my eye as another black SUV pulled up behind her. But this was no crazed killer. This was no weapon of war. The rear doors opened and two of the most beautiful looking people I'd ever seen stepped out.

Long blonde hair and beautiful blue eyes. They were dressed in shorts and t-shirts, with brown tanned skin.

"Mom?" Ava called out behind me. "Dad?"

But as soon as she said the words the crazed Commissioner's wife lunged, grabbing hold of Ava's mom to drag her closer.

"Connie!" Ava's dad roared. His eyes flew wide as he saw the mess of wires and explosives now pressed against his wife as he held up his hands and screamed. *"No!"*

A convoy of cars turned the corner and pulled to a stop on either side of Ava's parents' car. Doors opened. I caught sight of the Judge and Slayer, and then Brylee and Thorin...and then Balefire.

I sagged under the sight. Not him...not Balefire.

And behind him stepped the thirty-strong Hellhound army of guards.

"Here we are," the Judge murmured as he lifted his gaze to the towering building, and then the Commissioner's wife. "Who do we have here?"

"Neil Jordain," Slayer muttered. "That's the wife."

The way he said it—'*the wife*'—as though she had no name, no identity of her own, as if she was just *there*. It pissed me off.

I moved down the steps, tearing out of Nero's grip. "She's not just *the* wife. She's a woman, a *mortal*. You might've tricked the entire city into thinking I killed her husband, but one day the truth will come out."

The Judge never looked at me, only the frantic woman. "There's evidence she did it. You've seen the footage. You know she did."

And the woman seemed to shake and shudder, clutching Ava's mom in her arms. "I saw it. I saw it all. I know she did it. You told me she did. You showed me the evidence and told me where they'd be."

Dad gave a snarl behind me. "You knew she'd do something like this."

The Judge just gave a sickening smile. "I had hoped," he answered and then lowered his gaze to her. "Do it. This is what you came for, to exact revenge on the Vampire who killed your husband."

He looked at me, dark eyes bore right through me and I was back in that courtroom once more with terror and blood shed all around.

"I can't live like this, seeing my Neil's body when I'm asleep and when I'm awake," she stammered and gripped the button in her hand. "I can't do it."

"Then end it." The Judge stepped backwards, as did others.

My pulse thumped too fast.

The woman stilled, and then jerked her gaze to me. Everything happened in an instant. The Witches flew down the stairs around me as she dragged Ava's mom forward and then calmly lifted her hand, pointed at me...and then pressed the detonator.

CHAPTER FOURTEEN

MY WORLD WENT BOOM

Magic pricked over my skin like thousands of spider bites, piercing my flesh. I flinched, my eyes glued to the tragedy unfolding.

"Mom!" Ava shoved past, but I grabbed her arm and forced her against me. She tripped, stumbling toward me, a terrifying fear sweeping over her face, tears soaking her cheeks. I held her tight, her head pressed into the crook of my neck. She couldn't see this... she fucking couldn't. She shuddered against me, crying so loud.

Electricity speared out from the witches' fingertips at lighting speed. Racing. Racing. Racing. Slamming and smothering around Ava's mom, tearing her out from the Commissioner's wife's grip, and hurled her into the air and across the yard. Her screams were swallowed by Ava's.

In a terrible flash of fierce reds and oranges, the bomb strapped to the commissioner's wife exploded.

Boom!

Ava and I were ripped apart by the shock, leaving everyone stumbling.

A ball of blood and fire burst outward... tearing through the air like a great beast, growing, growling, ready to devour everything. The world seemed move so goddamn slowly, stealing all the good and innocence in me. The dreadful sound of the explosion renting the air.

I saw bits of flesh, a hand, pieces of fabric, and fiery shrapnel encased in a massive ball of flames coming for everyone.

I couldn't move... Couldn't. Screams rang in my ears while terror froze me to the spot, stealing my confidence and everything I believed in. It left me with a single thought... everything I'd fought for, I cried for, I'd die for, funneled down to one thing... Those I loved. I saw them in my mind's eyes slipping through my fingers.

Taken.

My scream was raw and frightful, clawing at my insides as my life flashed before my eyes. The ground quivered, and Anarchy released its cries.

All in a sliver of a second...

In the next instant, the explosive fire hit an invisible barrier around the commissioner's wife, rattling the ground, rebounding against a massive magic bubble.

Blue shards of power hurled from Tagar's palms, zigzagged over the explosive firestorm that swallowed the commissioner's wife inside, inhaling her completely.

No shock wave came... contained by the magical dome.

I stumbled at the top of the stairs, Ava darted down the steps to her mom, while I stood amid the chaos, agony shredding me. *What the fuck had I just seen?* My mind refused to make sense of it, refused to admit I'd just seen a woman blow herself up in front of me... I wasn't her enemy, never had been... The monsters stood behind her, they pulled her puppet strings, they controlled her life, and in the end, decided when to cut those strings.

The High Priest shook, his face pale, his eyes inky black as he fought to restrain the explosion.

Chaotic turmoil surrounded me, voices, screams, petrified people. The fire within the bubble sparked and snapped, bellowing and leaving nothing behind.

Tagar's Witches flanked him, their arms jutting outward, a rippled wave of energy shooting into the ball, taming the flaring flames that licked at the edges, seeking escape.

Soon, the fiery mass dissolved, ash falling to the ground, piling into mounds around the charred pieces of what once belonged to the commissioner's wife.

Clenching my jaw, I looked away, unable to stare at what had become of her.

"She's gone," Judas whispered in my ear, his arms holding me up on wobbly legs. "It was her choice."

I shook my head, tears welling in the corners. "What I just saw can never be wiped from my mind. Ever!"

He held me tight in his embrace, and tears fell, as they did for so many around me, for a woman who wanted to harm us, for a lost soul who grieved, for a desperate wife who listened to the monsters.

And that evil still lingered... Right on our doorstep, coming to destroy all of us. I broke from Judas and wiped my eyes.

"The fight has just started," he murmured, and he was right. So freaking right, I straightened my spine and nodded.

Ava and her parents darted up the stairs, the rest of their clan following, all under the watchful eyes of the Witches who were the only thing standing between us and the Council's lackeys. It wouldn't last, not for long, not when the enemy's army appeared larger.

With trembling arms, I waved everyone back inside. Dad was there, adding his voice to mine. "Move inside, quickly."

Ava's eyes were raw and red, but her lips pulled from ear to ear in a smile. She grasped onto her mom's arm and with the Witches who now retreated too, they poured into Anarchy.

Tagar marched up the stairs, his eyes filled with sorrow. He'd saved us, but took front stage at seeing a horrific death. He met my gaze and gave a tight nod, knowing that this had only just began. My emotions were jagged, and numbness took over my body, working on pure adrenaline, and I hoped, prayed we'd find a way for our side to win.

"Thank you," I said.

"I did what had to be done." He motioned toward his coven, urging them inside with a sweep of his hand.

Outside, a bitter wind coiled around me, tugging on my hair, but for those few moments the clouds and smoke parted. Sunlight beamed down on us. It warmed my shoulders and face, and I squinted against its brightness. More than anything I wanted to close my eyes, pretend I was back at the Academy where things were simple. Where I laughed with Ava, where my stomach swirled with butterflies in the Wolves' company. Where my biggest problem was dealing with Nesrin being a bitch.

"It's beautiful," I murmured.

"It's the eye of the storm," Judas added as he stepped alongside me.

"Calm before chaos ensues," Nero piped in, joining us along with Bond, who covered his eyes as he looked up.

"It's an omen," Tagar snarled. "A trick by the devil to

lure you out. Dangerous hours lie ahead of us all. Let's go inside where it's safe for now."

I swallowed hard, trying not to let his words make me feel worse, but when my gaze fell on the army below, also staring at the sudden parting of the heavens, my stomach clenched.

My attention searched the enormous ocean of supernaturals who wanted us dead, gone from this world, and halted on my principal. A powerful Hellhound. Balefire.

He wasn't staring into the sky, but looking directly at me, his gaze so dark I couldn't make out his expression from my distance.

I choked on air tainted by the stench of the explosive. He'd betrayed us, and that sat like a mountain in my gut... Had he hated me that much? I understood everyone else's hatred, but Balefire's was a spear to my heart. I'd thought he was on my side.

"Mor, let's go in," Judas murmured, his hand slipping from mine as he retreated with Nero and Bond. Tagar was gone too, and I remained in the doorway, facing a freaking army.

Behind them, the city burned in a sea of oranges and reds and blacks, smoke tendrils reaching for the sky, trying to escape.

There was nowhere else to go, no place to run or hide. This was where the final showdown would take place. What the council intended all along, to smoke us out of our hiding places, to destroy us. But had they anticipated so many would band together against them?

The endless army seemed to come over the horizon like a tsunami, about to engulf everything in their path. A chill traveled down my spine.

I stepped backwards and then turned, seeking the

protection of Anarchy while Judas and Nero shut the doors with a loud thud. A storm of voices hummed behind me, and the air grew thick with fear and tension.

A whistle sliced through the clamor, bringing everyone to silence. My dad was standing a few steps up on the staircase, drawing everyone's attention. Seeing him there, tall and proud and taking his position as leader, was the Dad I remembered. Something small cheered inside me to have him back, to know I faced this with him. Mom remained at the base of the stairs, holding onto the curled banister, and Vasile staggered up to join Dad, clear his old form was frail and injured.

"This isn't something I say lightly, or something I'd ever wished to say in my lifetime." He sighed heavily, shadows crawling under his eyes, but he never lowered his gaze or showed weakness. Not my dad.... Never my dad. "The Supernatural Council wish to stamp us out, eliminate every one of us. Your children, cousins, grandparents, friends. Everyone you hold dear. They've already destroyed our homes. So, our time to stand together is now. There's nowhere else to run."

Murmurs spread across the enormous hall, most nodding, some huddling their children close. My heart went to them, it killed me to see them scared they'd lose those precious to them.

The Ancient cleared his throat, raising his gaze to stare out to all those who banded to fight against the evil. "A fight is our last resort."

My stomach hurt, having seen first-hand the ugliness of the council's intentions, but running straight into a fight, a war cry on my lips wasn't the answer either.

You're smart, I know you'll figure it out. Dad's words

skimmed my brain. He always fought with his wits first, and he'd do the same now.

"What are we meant to do now?" someone else called out.

"Prepare for war," Dad answered.

CHAPTER FIFTEEN

A PLAN IS BORN

"I don't like this," I murmured and looked to Dad.

He was still hurt, still shaking and weak. Slayer filled my mind. He was a killing machine, a deadly killing machine. Dad was no match for him if it came down to that.

"But we prepare ourselves. We wait," Dad stated. He glanced to the Ancient, who nodded.

I looked to the front of Anarchy. The building would hold...for a while. But what then? What happens when the walls crumble and the magic escapes? What happens when those I love...those too weak to fight back fall to their knees.

My thoughts turned to Balefire and his men, and I felt again that plunge of betrayal. There had to be a reason for him to take the Council's side. There had to be.

If I could talk to him, explain what was really happening, then he'd understand...then maybe he'd take our side. I had to get out there, had to see if there was a way to talk to him, without getting myself killed.

I glanced to Judas and the others. He met my gaze, his brow narrowed like he already knew what was in my head.

Creepy. Ava glanced my way as I moved. She untangled herself from her Mom's arms and took a step toward me.

"What is it?" She glanced to the Wolves as we met them.

"I can't understand Balefire's allegiance to that slimy piece of shit," I murmured and shook my head. "I just can't. There has to be a reason he's taken the Council's side on this. There has to be."

"So what, you want to try to figure this out on our own?" Nero glanced to the others.

"No, I want to talk to him. I want to understand what we're really up against here."

"You're crazy," Bond growled and shook his head before he took a step closer, keeping his snarl low so others couldn't hear. "You see how many are out there? We can't even get close to the guy, and you want to what have a tête-à-tête with the guy?"

I flinched with his anger. We were all dancing on egg shells here, and searching for the damn cracks. "Balefire is the key to us winning this thing. I know it. He has the strength and the numbers and if you're prepared to go head to head with him without trying your damnedest to upend the scales in our favor, then you're not thinking straight."

They all fell silent and sucked in a hard breath.

"She's right," Nero murmured. "With Balefire we have a chance at winning...and when I mean winning, I mean staying alive."

"And how do you suggest we do this?" Judas growled and glanced to his second.

"We create a diversion." Ava glanced to her parents. "That's all you need, right? A diversion to get to the Principal? Then you can talk to him, try to get him to our side?"

"Yeah." I nodded, trying to think. "It's all we have right now."

"We need Nesrin." Ava turned to find the Panther and waved her over.

"What do you want now?" she snarled, striding towards us.

Her lips curled as Ava motioned her closer still. She gave a huff and then leaned in.

"You said this place was in the middle of the stormwater pipes, right?"

"Yeah," she muttered. "So?"

"We've had a lot of rain lately." Ava kept on her train of thought. "I bet there's a lot of water still running through those pipes."

We all waited for her to make her point.

"We can control the water," she murmured. "Dad can. He can make it rise to the surface, we can flood them."

I stood there, stunned.

"It might work," Judas murmured and glanced to me. "If Ava can make enough of a diversion, then Balefire and the others might scatter."

"And give me enough time to talk to him." I gave a nod. "It's worth a shot."

Bond glanced to the others, and I followed his gaze, taking in the Witches, the Wolves, the Panthers and the Great Creatures of the Sea. They were all here, everyone we loved...everyone we cared for.

"If anyone else has a better idea, then now would be the time," I muttered and turned back to our circle.

I was determined to be different, to not just make the decisions about me, to be humble and kind, and stand strong...*together*.

"Let's do this." Bond nodded. "It's a solid idea, better than the fistful of nothing we had before.

"Then we need to tell our parents," Ava muttered. "And hope like Hell they agree."

I sucked in a hard breath. She was right. Convincing Judas and the others was the easy part. They were used to my crazy schemes, but Mom and Dad? That was another thing altogether.

I strode toward them. Dad was talking to Chuck, and his men, Mom glanced my way and gave me a small smile.

"Everything okay, honey?" she murmured.

Dad turned toward me as I started to speak, "I think I have a way to shut this attack down."

Mom jerked a careful glance to Dad, as she always did.

"I'm listening." Dad's gaze slipped to the others behind me.

I didn't need to turn my head to know Ava and the others were doing the exact same thing. I sucked in a breath and started. "I... *I mean, we* think if we can get to Principal Balefire, then we can get him to side with us instead of the Council."

There was a pause, a second where if I had a heartbeat it might've stopped dead before sadness swept across Dad's face. He shook his head. "The Council owns the Hellhounds, Mor. Their allegiance has always been the law."

My stomach sank with his words. "No," I murmured and shook my head. "I don't believe that. I know Principal Balefire, he helped me...helped me hide. He helped me escape."

One brow shot high on Dad's face. "He did? You never told me that."

"I didn't think it was important. I mean, he was all ally to a point."

I had Dad's full interest now. He crossed his arms over his chest and glanced to Chuck. "Tell me more about this *point*."

I resurrected the memories of that night in the rain, giving Dad all the information I could.

"He gave you safety and protection, but nothing more," Dad murmured. "Nothing that would be seen as an outright stance against the Council...*interesting*."

"So there's a crack in his alliance." I urged. "And where there's a crack, there's a way in."

He seemed to think about this for a long time before he glanced to Chuck. No words were needed. It was as though they held a private conversation inside their heads....until finally Chuck murmured. "It's something we need to explore. If we can stop this without going to war..."

"I agree." Dad turned to me. Pride welled in his eyes. "I don't know when it happened, but you've become a brilliant strategist, and a steadfast leader. I'm so proud of you. So proud of the Vampire you've become."

An ache swelled inside my chest. I swallowed, glancing at Chuck who looked at me with the same blinding love Dad did. "I want to say thank you. I want to hold you close, to hug you and Mom and Chuck and all my friends. But I'm going to take a raincheck on that. When this is all over, I'm going to take all the hugs I can get."

"It's a deal," Dad said and smiled.

I turned to the others, watching as Ava's Dad glanced this way and then slowly nodded.

"It looks like you have your chance," Dad murmured and stepped forward.

We seemed to meet in the middle, Ava's parents on one side, and mine on the other.

"You okay with this?" Dad looked to Ava's father.

"I can do it." He glanced to the front of the building. "I just hope the building here can take a little water."

"Well," Dad sighed. "Looks like we're about to find out."

Nesrin's Dad leaned close and whispered to her Mom, then she turned, walked toward the Wolves, and before we knew it, everyone in Anarchy had heard about our plans. They gathered in groups and headed toward us.

"We want to help," Nesrin's Mom stated. "Just tell us what to do and we'll do it."

Ava's dad looked her and then the others. "We need you to be ready if this doesn't go well. I'll try and keep the waters from invading the chapel, but we need those who are weakest ready to leave."

"Leave where?" Nesrin's Mom looked to the others. "Most of us have lost our homes...most have lost everything."

"I don't know." He just shook his head. "I wish I had the answer. Tell the others to run and hide if they can. Those who can will stand and fight." Ava's dad glanced to me. "We're placing a lot on such young shoulders."

"I can do it." My voice was croaky and hoarse. "I know I can."

"Very well." Ava's Dad gave a nod and turned to mine. "When you're ready. We'll need to go outside...and begin."

I didn't know what *begin* meant exactly. But, I turned to the others. Ava walked toward me, taking my arm and leading me to the Wolves.

"We can draw Slayer and the Judge to one side, while you do your best to draw Balefire toward you," Bond said.

The plan seemed simple; divide and beg and plead and hope to God that I could get through to Balefire before he turned on me.

Murmurs cut through the rest of the crowd. Nesrin's

mom moved from group to group, ushering the old and the frail into smaller groups with one stronger person in each group.

I took a second, finding my way through them to press my hand against the stony walls of Anarchy, and whispered to the building. "I'm going to need you one last time. I know you protected them before, but do you think you can do it again?"

There was no whisper of darkness this time, no breath of cold against my skin. I whispered a silent prayer.

Ava's dad kissed her Mom, and then turned to the Ancient. "For old time's sake."

Vlad Vasile gave a slow nod. My own dad followed them out to the front of Anarchy once more. He gave me a nod, one that said *do your best*.

CHAPTER SIXTEEN

SHARK WEEK

"God, this has to work," Judas murmured in my ear, and with Ava, the three of us huddled outside, near the corner of Anarchy. Shadows from the nearby trees crowded the building and concealed us as we stared out to the massive army. Bond, Nero, and several other Wolf shifters were hiding on the other side of the building in the opposite corner, a distraction should we need it when it was time to run.

Seeing the sheer mass ahead of us terrified me. They'd come here with one mission, one frightful purpose... to eliminate our families out of existence.

My hands balled into fists, fury surging through me.

We waited for the chaos to start. We counted on it to throw the Council's army into disarray. We needed Balefire. He'd tip the fight in our favor, and failure wasn't an option.

"It'll work," Ava snarled. "You wait and see. My parents will more than deliver." Her smugness made me smile. She was so proud of her family, and knowing they were safe had rekindled the fire in her eyes.

"It will," I confirmed. "I know it will." *Oh, please let this work.*

"There," Judas whispered, pointing to a storm sewer at the side of the street, far enough from the army who were too preoccupied with staring at Anarchy, waiting for instructions, to notice.

Water pooled out of the drains, moving slowly like outstretched hands, eddying against the natural incline of the curb.

Rushing outward silently, no one noticed the water, no one paid attention.

Judge stood up front, shoulders wide, head high, his mouth twisted as he glanced up at Anarchy, eyes filled with mania and hunger, and he wore that sickening smile again. He was young... not much older than me, and yet he'd clawed his way to that position and craved so much power. He held not a thread of mercy. I saw it on his face, like I had when he'd pushed the commissioner's wife into taking her life, and when he'd ordered my dad...

You will succumb to my demands and pick a fucking side!

But it was never a choice for Dad, and Judge knew it.

Slayer stood near him, stoic as always, darkness stealing his expression, both of them in a whispered conversation. Brylee and Thorin were farther back, but my gaze found Balefire, his pack of Hellhound warriors standing tall behind him.

Now it was time for him to make a decision. He'd helped me evade the Council before when he didn't need to. So, why would he fight against me now? The ringing in my gut—instinct—screamed this was my chance to make him reconsider.

We waited in our hiding spot in silence, my eyes glued

to the other storm drains, bubbling, overflowing, pushing outward.

"It's going to take too long?" I muttered. "No one's gonna stand there while it slowly floods. We need—"

"Just wait and you'll see," Ava cut me off. "Be ready because once it happens, everyone will panic. And that's your chance."

I nodded, pressing my shoulder to the wall, staring at them, waiting as nerves chewed on my confidence.

The ground quivered beneath us, and we all exchanged glances, while Ava smiled wildly, nodding her head like this was the big moment.

Up ahead, the army wobbled on their feet, feeling the jolt, realizing that something was wrong. They looked around with puzzled expressions.

Slayer swung in a sudden jolt, his mouth open with a command, an arm in the air, but his words were stolen.

Water surged out of the gutters like a fountain, the metal grating flinging into the air in an explosive show. Turbid brown water... all dirty and gross, came spewing out endlessly, shooting into the air, spreading its grasp.

My heart pounded at how fast it all happened. The army ran in every direction, lost and chaotic, Judge and Slayer were completely drenched, but they were yelling something, knowing this wasn't a freak accident.

The gurgling and growling from the deluge swallowed every other sound.

People ran in every direction, unsure how to stop the torrential attack.

The street vanished under the rising tides.

Water rushed onto the front yard of Anarchy, lapping against the front steps, curling around our feet. Up ahead, it rose over the streets with such speed, it terrified me.

The soup of brown water and debris swirled, looking for a place to go. Several of the army lost their footing and wailed as they fell in, swept away by the torrent that kept coming, gushing out of the drains like a burst damn. I loved Ava's family right then!

"Now!" Ava cried in my ear. "Go!"

My muscles flexed, gaze sweeping the chaos, searching for Balefire. My mind raced as panic gripped me.

"I can't find him," I blurted.

The swell on the street grew. The army moved in every direction, looking for a solution, a way out. Anything to make sense of the chaotic onslaught.

A flash of movement, and I spotted him, pushing through the liquid rising to his knees, the cascade soaking him to the bone.

I burst forward, not waiting another second.

Movement to my right as Nero, Bond, and the other Wolves emerged, sliding forward, hiding behind trees, ready to jump in if shit went sideways. Using the line of trees flanking the front yard, I moved with speed, water sloshing and splashing across my knees. But no one would notice, not when water still spurted out of the drains. Nothing would stop me... not even the reek of the putrid water. Nothing.

Behind me Ava and Judas stayed close, their breathing heavy, and panic stifled the air. Up ahead, Balefire raced to his pack and grasped the arm of someone submerged under water.

Judge bellowed, and his words reached me. "Attack!"

Fear gripped me, and I had to move fast. I felt nothing, numbness taking me over, and I ran on pure adrenaline now. This was how warriors must feel during battles, rushing in head first, all pumped. Feeling nothing but the need to destroy, fear vanishing.

Judge yelled again, but very few heard him over the rushing sound of water, the wails and confusion.

Good. Fucking excellent.

This was my chance, and I peeled out from behind the tree and moved fast, head low, but eyes on the prize. Balefire wrenched one of his men from the moving river that twisted and tore down the sloped road, away from Anarchy. But the waters were deeper here, reaching my thighs.

Judge screamed something else, but I kept my focus dead ahead.

In a heartbeat, there was a splash several feet in front of me, movement under water, and a shadow... a five-foot shadow, glided past. A fin, gray blue, emerged and sliced through the water.

My brain stuttered for a moment as I took a double take, unsure how to feel right now. "I-is t-hat a fucking shark?"

"Oh, that's just my cousin, Jon," Ava murmured like she spoke of going to high tea with her cousin. She leaned down and shoved her face in the water then started screaming commands.

Judas and I exchanged confused glances before turning back to Ava.

All I could hear was, "Blub-blub-blubbbbb!"

She pulled her head out of the water, swinging wet hair off her face like one of those bikini models. Then she looked my way. "What?"

"What?" I was shaking my head.

"This is a goddamn shit show," Judas blurted.

Ava turned to him and bellowed, "It's a goddamn SHARK SHOW, that's what it is!! Go Aunty June!!"

I followed her line of sight to another shark lunging out

of the water and latching onto a man's arm, then dragging him under. His friend spun around to find him gone, only a bloom of blood spreading across the water. He screamed, panic blanching his face as he rushed in the opposite direction.

"Fuck!" Judas murmured.

Thank Hell, Ava was on our side. I refocused.

Balefire.

He lingered up ahead, looking anything but his calm self; frazzled, lost and confused.

"Bitch," someone growled, and we all turned to our right to find one of the men from the Judge's army. The man towered over us with shoulders to carry the world. Not waiting for a second, he charged.

My stomach dropped, and I spun to face him. But Judas threw himself at the newcomer, slamming into him, a fist to the face. They crumbled and fell into the water with a splash when someone else grabbed my arm with such force, I stumbled backward, losing my balance.

"I have you now!" he snarled.

I hit the water, the chill swallowing me. In a flash, he released his grip on me, and I splashed and pushed myself to my feet, fists curled, ready to fight, when a tentacle snapped toward his face, slamming him so hard he flung backward.

Ava stood there, heaving, another tentacle sliding out from under her shirt, the fabric straining, and her face serious. Deadly serious.

"Go!" she demanded.

So I did, pushing one leg after another through the water that seems to have a power of its own, somehow feeling thicker than it should. My head spun with the movement all around me, the Sea Creatures already in warfare mode, waging their own battle, attacking unannounced, taking them down, one at a time.

Up ahead, Balefire had his back to me, and I had to reach him.

Some ran past me, one man's face in the grip of horror, a shark's fin carving the water's surface, racing after him. His screams flooded the air, but I didn't look back, couldn't.

Up ahead, the army came into view as they pushed forward to charge Anarchy, a wall of them that would crush anyone in their way.

A scream wedged in my throat, the terror of their onslaught throttling me.

I swung toward Balefire, pushing, moving faster. His name grazing my throat as the roar of the army came again.

Dread rose through me. I stood in the middle of the enemy on a whim, on a hope, and I couldn't even reach Balefire. Too much distance lay between us, along with men and their hatred.

I didn't stop though. My breath rushed when I caught heavy eyes on me, leaving me shivering. Lifting my head, I glanced over to the far right, closer to Anarchy. Judge stood there.

Watching me.

He'd seen me.

He'd fucking seen me.

CHAPTER SEVENTEEN

THE ULTIMATE SACRIFICE

"Balefire!" I roared, lifting my feet to charge through the water just as Slayer burst through the surface to our left. "Balefire, *please!*"

Slayer gasped and spluttered, stumbled sideways. His shirt was missing, and there was a savage bite mark on his arm, but it was already healing, leaving pale skin to sparkle with the water.

"Slayer!" Judge roared and pointed at me, drawing the Vampire's attention.

Chaos reigned as Ava's dad still called the fury of the seas and the water obeyed rising higher...and higher...and higher. But my focus was on the one person who mattered the most right now.

"Principal Balefire!" I screamed.

But it was Slayer who turned, and it was Slayer who curled his lips in excitement. I glanced around in a panic and took a step backwards.

"Now...where the fuck were we, you little bitch," Slayer growled as a fin came up out of the water.

But this time he was ready. In one fluid motion he

turned, raised his fist and struck. The shark slapped its tail against the surface as the blow connected. Balefire turned behind the Vampire, and watched as Slayer hauled the mammoth shark out of the water and hurled it through the air.

The shark hit the surface with a *splash* before Slayer turned and focused those deadly eyes on me.

"Wait!" The Ancient stumbled toward Judge, his hands out. "Stop this insanity. I beg you...please, listen to reason."

I jerked my gaze to Slayer, and then to the Ancient as he fell to his knees in front of the Judge.

But there was no pause as the Judge reached for his waist and dragged a dagger free. I could see it all as Vlad's eyes widened, his gaze seized by the point of the knife.

Panic roared, tearing through me like lightning. *"No! Wait!"* I lunged toward them, stumbling in the water, only to punch my feet against the flooded asphalt.

And in one fatal, terrifying arc, the Judge plunged the knife down and into the Ancient's chest.

"No...*no...no...no!*" I screamed.

Slayer was coming for me, tearing through the water. I couldn't reach the Ancient in time. I knew I couldn't. Then with an unmerciful howl, Balefire roared. "Protect Morwenna!"

He lunged into the air, driving massive thighs through the rising sea. His men stopped fighting, one by one, and turned toward their leader. And just like that, there was the turn of the tide.

Hellhound hunted Vampire...who hunted me. All I could see was the Ancient falling...all I could see was the end. I stumbled forward as Slayer grunted, plunging through the last fifteen feet to get to me.

I tore my gaze to Balefire, the words slipping from my lips. "It's okay. You tried. It's okay."

Somewhere amongst the fighting I heard Judas scream. "Morwenna...*NO!*"

Stars collided in Slayer's eyes, he reached out his hand, fingers ready to grab and hurt and kill until the blur of darkness rushed toward him, knocking him sideways.

Slayer grabbed my wrist and pulled me with him. My knees buckled with the force. Water was all I knew as I was sucked under and rolled. Hands and fists swung out, before burning red eyes filled my view.

I kicked and shoved, seeing Balefire reach for the henchman. Terror held me under as Slayer pulled me closer. Legs and feet and a circling shark filled my view. But there he was, his long pale hair like strands of a whip.

Balefire grabbed him from behind, arms wrapped around his chest as the Hellhound tried to heave him backwards. But his grip was a vise around my wrist and there was no letting go.

"No...get off me!"

Power surged from my chest, dark power...hungry power. It kicked like a mule, tearing Slayer's grip free and shoving me backwards through the rush of water. I punched my feet down, finding the asphalt and shot upwards.

Water rushed into my nose with the breath. I coughed, spluttered and then looked around. The Ancient was there, floating face down in the water, arms outspread like he was bodysurfing through the ripples. Dad let out a scream, his hands around the Judge's neck.

The knife slashed through the air as the Judge tried to kill the last man who stood in his way of power. That dark power rippled inside me. Here was the one responsible for all this death and destruction. Here was the most monstrous of us all.

I charged through the water as Slayer and Balefire splashed and kicked and then fell silent behind me. There was no looking back, no giving in to what had to be done to be free of them.

To be free of it all.

And with a howl of rage I speared Hekate's power through the air and into the piece of shit that had started this all. The Judge stilled, his eyes filled with darkness, and the knife slipped from his hand.

With a single *snap* of his neck he was falling, arms now limp at his side. His knees buckled before he slid into the water with barely a sound. The grey fin came out of nowhere, small beady black eyes, rows and rows of teeth reminding me of the razor wire around the compound as the Great White came up and out of the water and with one *chomp* took the Judge back down.

He was gone, just like that.

Gone in an instant, with Dad standing there looking at me like I'd been the one to save them all. The Ancient floated nearby and Dad rushed toward him as Balefire tore past me, heading for the leader of our line.

"Vlad!" Dad grabbed him, turning the Vampire over.

There was a blink, a slow blink, enough to let us know he was still alive. Black blood oozed from the gash in his chest. Pale lips parted, murmuring.

Balefire was close. He leaned in, grabbed one side of the Ancient as Dad grasped the other. But Vlad's words called them closer. They both leaned in, dripping water over the Ancient's chest.

I couldn't hear them, standing there stunned while Balefire's men took care of the last of the Council members.

Something smacked into my leg and I looked down to find Slayer staring up into nothing. Half of his face, his throat, and his chest had been burned, leaving nothing but a charred hole behind. I had to think to myself what kind of power does something like that? What kind of hunger burns like liquid lava under ten inches of water?

A Hellhound did.

One who was pissed off and now fighting for the right side.

I glanced toward them as the Ancient's lips stopped moving. Dad lifted his head. His dark, careful eyes met mine as his brow rose. Balefire looked at me with the same expression, and then with a small, brittle gasp...the Ancient was gone.

His body turned brittle and broke away, hitting the water before it turned to ash. There was no body to mourn over, nothing so neat and perfect, just specks of grey that washed away as the others stilled all around me.

"Mor?" Judas called, wading through the water to get to me. "Mor."

He pulled me into his arms. "Thank Lucifer you're okay."

But I wasn't okay. I didn't think I'd ever be okay. Never again.

I watched the last bits of the Ancient float away and then glanced to my dad. That could've been him...that could've been us all. Floating...forgotten. Tears filled my eyes as I turned to my Wolves.

Nero and Bond were there, rushing through the water to get to me. They held me. I held them, grasping tight to what was warm and real and when I finally found the strength to speak, I whispered, "Get me out of this damn water."

Judas gave a chuckle, bent and slid one hand under my knees. I didn't know how the water slipped away from us. All I knew was the relief of climbing those stairs to the old, run down chapel and a sense of ease.

"You okay?" Bond searched my face with his fingers and then swept them down my arm. "I thought for sure Slayer had you."

I glanced to Balefire and answered, "He did."

But then I was saved...saved by Balefire and Ava and my Wolves and my Dad. I was saved by them all.

"It's over," Judas murmured and pressed his face into the crease of my neck. "It's all over, they can never hurt us again."

Bodies lay on the bitumen. One lone shark, three Wolves and someone else I didn't know. That was four bodies too many. "I want this to stop. I want this to all stop, all the rage and the hate." I lifted my gaze to Judas. "I want there to be peace and compassion."

Dad looked at me, like he was hanging on every word I said.

"I know," Judas murmured and smoothed the sodden strands of my hair against my back. "It will now...we can finally move on."

Those inside Anarchy spilled out through the doorway, Wolves, Witches, and Vampires standing together as one.

"I'm so proud of you," Dad spoke. "All of you. The way you were out there, I've never seen anyone so determined to protect and save. You made me proud."

"You've made all of us proud," Ava's dad agreed.

I glanced to my best friend and held out my hand. Ava dropped her arm from around Chuck and gripped my fingers. We were one...this bunch of misfits and weirdos.

Vampire. Wolf. Great Creature of the Sea.

We shouldn't have worked, but somehow, we did.

"Let's get this cleaned up," Balefire growled and turned his head, giving commands to his Hellhound guards.

"Thank you, Principal Balefire." He stilled and then glanced my way when I spoke. "We wouldn't have won without you."

"No, you wouldn't. But we were never against you, Mor. All good things come to those who wait." There was a sly smile before he spoke again. "And I think we can drop the Principal now, don't you?"

He cut a secret glance to Dad and then turned away, leaving me wondering what exactly he meant.

"He's right," Dad muttered and reached for Mom's hand. "It is time to clean all this up. We'll start with a press conference, clearing your name, Morwenna."

I flinched with the thought. Clearing my name.

And then what?

I didn't know...*but I was hopeful.*

Judas's hand tightened around mine as he whispered, "And you and I...and Bond and Nero are sneaking away for just a little while...just to breathe...just to touch and kiss and remember we're alive."

A shudder raced along my spine. I liked the sound of that...*very...very much.*

"Come here, you," Judas called.

My heart raced at the sound, panic surging just under the surface. It'd been days since the attack at Anarchy. Days since the end of it all, and in those days, there's been a new City born, a City filled with the first tremor of hope.

But I wasn't there yet.

I was still jumpy, still nervous...still looking over my shoulder.

Judas dropped the bags onto the oversized bed and stepped toward me. "It's okay. We're right here."

"She okay?" Bond carried another two bags in behind me. Anyone would think we were running away.

Maybe we were...would that be so bad? The idea took root inside me, turning the panic into something else...something that felt almost like excitement. "Yeah, I'm okay."

But Judas was worried. I could see it in his eyes. This getaway was his idea, escape into the woods where no one could find us.

Nero's phone beeped and he reached for his pocket.

"Ava again?" I murmured.

Nero just gave a smile, shook his head and texted back. "Only the tenth time since we left that she's checked on you."

I missed her already, missed her laughter, missed her crazy conversations—ones that were now directed to the future. I wanted to be there with her, thinking about the future, but I was still stuck in the past, unable to step forward.

Judas thought this was the way for me to do just that...step forward.

He moved closer, cutting across the beam of sunlight to get to me. My ring sparkled in the light, ruby red thrown against my pale skin, like blood. Warm lips grazed my knuckles.

"I was going to wait for tonight," Judas whispered against my skin. "But I think we've waited long enough, don't you?"

He lifted his gaze, but it wasn't me he looked at...it was the others. Bags hit the floor...floorboards groaned under their weight. Nero touched me, brushing strands of my hair from my shoulder and leaned in to kiss the side of my neck.

"Don't look back there," Judas murmured. "Not in the past. Just stay right here, for a while at least. Stay with us."

Bond reached around, sliding his hand along my hip and then around to my stomach. But it was Judas I watched as the Alpha stepped closer, towering over me, and leaned down.

His lips brushed mine as Bond reached upwards, cupping my breast. I loved them...every one of them, they fulfilled me in ways I couldn't understand and right now, I didn't want to.

Warmth at my neck, and my breast, delving into my

mouth. Judas lifted his hands to the small buttons of my top. I trembled, this time not with fear—but with anticipation.

I lowered one hand to my side and reached for him. Bond's thigh tensed under my touch as I gripped his jeans and pulled him closer. My fangs nipped the inside of my mouth, and I felt Judas's tongue dance around the pointed end before he pulled away.

The lick of my top lip made me shudder and close my eyes.

"We're going to take such good care of you," Judas whispered as the buttons of my top opened.

They pulled away from me for a second. Fabric skimmed my arms. I opened my eyes, standing before them in my jeans and bra. One soft pinch at the middle of my back and the straps of that too slipped over my shoulders.

Goosebumps raced across my skin as Judas lowered his head and took the peak of my breast into his mouth. Nero's fingers traced my cheek, before he turned my head, hungry for my mouth. I lost myself in the feel of them. In the pop of my button and the zipper sliding low.

Before I knew it I was standing there naked. Feather light touches, the slow slide of a tongue. Blue eyes called me as Judas rose from the floor and dropped my panties to the ground.

He reached over his shoulder and pulled his shirt free. Bond was already hurrying, shirt gone, frantic fingers working the button of his jeans. I slid my hand over the denim, fingers finding the length of his desire and he moaned into my ear. "Hell, I missed you."

I broke the kiss, looking into Nero's gaze, and then Judas as I gripped Bond. "I missed you too."

Judas lifted me like I weighed nothing at all and carried me to the bed. This was the first time we'd been together—

all of us together and not just sleeping and comforting. Bed springs howled under the weight as Nero and Bond followed.

Mouths blended into one. I lost track of their movements. Fingers touched, lips kissed...and their tongues... I lowered my hand, speared my fingers through Judas' hair as he licked my breast.

"I love you." The words vibrated against my skin. He lifted his head, blue eyes sparkling with the truth. "I've always loved you, Morwenna."

"Me too." Nero moved in, mouth greedy for mine. The kiss was electric and hungry.

"Me too." Bond leaned in to kiss the inside of my thigh.

"Can you handle that?" Judas growled. "Three demanding Wolves, and when I say demanding, I mean we plan on making this beautiful body hum all night long."

Bond moved deeper, mouth wanting, fingers searching as he licked between my crease. A whimper tore from my lips.

"I'm gonna take that as a yes." Judas chuckled.

I slid my hand from his hair to skim the muscles of his shoulders and then lower. He rose, letting me touch where I wanted to touch. And I wanted it all. I wanted all of them, as much as I could, as hard and as fast as I could. I wanted to drown myself in the feel of them, underneath me, on top of me, pressing me down until they were all I could feel.

The lick to my core made me shudder. Bond gave a groan of delight and the sound vibrated against my tender flesh. Heat tore through me, and in the quiet, lonely place inside my chest my heart gave a *thud*...and then another.

I opened my eyes at the sensation. Bond stilled. Nero broke the kiss to lean backwards. "You okay?"

Thud...thud...thud... There was a rhythm, a flow...a

newness inside me. My lips curled into a smile. "I'm more okay right here than I have been in a very long time."

"We can stay if you want?" Nero leaned close and murmured against my lips. "We can stay here forever."

I smiled, reached up to grasp the back of his neck and pulled him closer, kissing him until Judas licked my breasts and Bond delved deeper than ever before, until my body trembled with pent up release.

Bond pulled away, shoving the rest of his clothes to the floor. I slid my hand to Judas, and curled my fingers around the length of his cock. He moaned, thrusting his hips, pumping against my hand as Nero rose.

His erection stood straight up from a thatch of thick midnight hair. I looked up at him...I'd never seen anyone so beautiful...Bond breached my walls. I trembled with the feel of him, parting my thighs wider as I drew Nero close.

Smooth against my tongue, Nero's cock slid deeper into my mouth. I was lost to the sensation as Bond pushed inside with a slow thrust. Judas growled, tongue greedy at my breast as he brushed his fingers against my other.

My body trembled, and the quake raced through me as Bond growled as well. The savage, possessive sounds of my Wolves echoing in the air around me as a climax tore free. I moaned against Nero, sliding my hand lower, taking more of him into my mouth as he pumped his hips.

His hand slid to my head, holding me steady as he took control. I thrust my hips upwards, meeting the slap of flesh as Judas pumped harder, wrapping his hand around mine, and pulled away at the last second. Warmth splashed against my breast at the same time as Bond gave a snarl and slammed home.

Nero pumped, pushing deeper, and deeper until the tendons of my jaw strained, and then he let go. I swallowed, my head buried against his body, until he shuddered and then eased his hold.

Spent and exhausted, they collapsed onto the bed next to me. Judas on one side, Nero on the other, Bond nestled between my thighs. Heavy, pants filled the room. But I was captured by the pulse in my head.

Soft pulse...

A calling pulse.

I lifted my hand, fingers slick in the wetness of my breast.

"You okay?" Judas murmured and rolled toward me.

"Give me your hand." I reached for it, pressing the tips of his fingers against my skin.

His eyes widened, brow shot high. "You have a heartbeat."

"How?" Nero jerked upwards, hand reaching, pressing against the middle of my chest. Bond reached over my body, and felt for the tremble.

"Holy shit," Nero murmured.

The dark power flickered inside me.

"What does this mean?" Bond asked.

I just shook my head. I didn't know if it was the Hekate's power or the fact that for the first time in what felt like forever...I was content.

We made love again after that, lazy love with Judas nestled against my back, and his cock between my thighs. We touched and we kissed, and we loved each other...until the sunlight slowly slipped away, until Nero rose from the bed, lit a candle and then walked out into the lounge room of the tiny one bedroom cabin and made a fire.

The sharp scent of smoke filled my nose as the darkness receded, giving way to an amber glow. Bond leaned forward, kissed me on the lips and murmured, "Don't know about you, but I'm starving."

He rose then, leaving Judas laying still and content. Pots and pans rattled, the sizzle of butter filled the air a second later. Judas gave a growl, shoved upwards and then stilled. "Pancakes...that's what we need."

"Already three steps ahead of you!" Bond called out.

"With bacon!" Nero added. "Lots and lots of bacon."

I chuckled at the sound of them...so *normal*.

Judas held out his hand and waited. "First shower's all yours, on the condition I get to wash your back."

I sighed, smiling harder than I've ever smiled before. "Deal."

"If you wash her back, I'm washing her front." Nero chuckled.

"And if you guys wash her back and her front, then I'm just gonna have to get her all dirty again," Bond growled from the doorway.

I rose from the bed and shook my head, laughter spilling from my lips.

This was how my life was going to be now. It wouldn't be all laughter and love, I knew that. But it would be with them and that was all that mattered.

"Deal," I answered and met each stare from my hungry...*hungry* Wolves.

www.ingramcontent.com/pod-product-compliance
Lightning Source LLC
Chambersburg PA
CBHW020819190726
48285CB00006B/2334